Messengers of Peace

Inspiring Stories of Africans Creating Peace

DeEtte Beghtol Waleed

*Waleed
Publications*

Printed in the United States.

Library of Congress Control Number: 2011916009

ISBN: 978-0-615-52888-5

1st Edition: November 2011

Front cover graphic provided courtesy of General Board of General Missions
United Methodist Church.
Cover design, page layout, and coaching for self-publishing by Kassy Daggett,
www.anthologypublishing.com, 541-683-1776, P.O. Box 518, Marcola, OR 97454
Editing by Victor Rozek, www.vrkd.com

Waleed Publications
deettebw@gmail.com
http://messengersofpeace-deette.blogspot.com
P.O. Box 30714
Portland, OR 97294

Praise for Messengers of Peace

"These stories are fascinating, important, true. Get beyond newspaper headlines and glimpse ordinary, contemporary individuals in Zambia by reading these stories. Leon, a privileged mayor in Congo, follows his conscience and promptly suffers the privations of a refugee camp. Another story describes the work being done with a rural population around the complex issue of Female Genital Mutilation."

—**Chris Adams,** Librarian

"Amidst the clutter and clatter of 'media-as-business' there remains a continuous clamor for drama that sells. The ills of Africa are often the favored narratives. Africa's disease

> **With every page you read, stories of boldness, strength and wisdom are being released. This is the hope for peace in Africa.**

pandemics, violent barbarism, collapsed nation-states and environmental disasters seem to be the special mentions of the day. Yet, across this vast, colorful, diverse and resilient continent, there are hosts of hidden heroes and heroines who are daily creating peace and with every act they are re-writing the script of violence and destruction. Often these stories are untold, silenced in the cacophony of bad news. This book provides us with an alternative text, one that highlights the remarkable work of the Messengers of Peace program in Zambia.

"DeEtte, who I had the personal privilege of working with for 6 years, is particularly well-positioned to be the mid-wife of these narratives as she has walked with the people of Africa leaving a gentle footprint. With every page you read, stories of boldness, strength and wisdom are being released. This is the hope for peace in Africa."

—**Carl Stauffer, Ph.D.,**
Assistant Professor of Justice & Development Studies
Center for Justice & Peacebuilding (CJP)
Eastern Mennonite University

"We understand that today there are some 10,000 Messengers of Peace. This is very commendable and is a tribute both to the messengers themselves and also to DeEtte Beghtol Waleed.

"It is not often that one is privileged to see the results of seeds planted some 22 years earlier, only to find that they have not only germinated but have sprouted wider than one could have imagined. The United Nations system under my leadership as Resident Coordinator in Zambia over the period 1998-2003, incorporated the Messengers of Peace into its Dag Hammarsjöld memorial initiative.

"International peace and security are not only timely, but in keeping with imperatives of the UNSCR 1325, which envisages the participation of women at the peace table."

—**Olubanke King-Akerele,**
former Minister of Foreign Affairs, Liberia,
and UN Resident Coordinator for Zambia

*"**Messengers of Peace** is precisely the book to recommend to students who have been victims of war, violence, oppression, and abuse, to show them that they are not alone in their quest, which is rapidly becoming a worldwide phenomenon. The greatest hope we, as a species, can have is an eternal spring of renewal powered by individuals, such as those profiled in the book, who commit their lives to fresh approaches to age-old conflicts.*

"As director of our graduate program in conflict resolution, I am fortunate to get to know students from around the world. They are attracted to our program because they want to help create a culture of peace, nonviolence, and conflict resolution back at home. On Orientation Day, I plan to have copies of this book on hand for both our domestic and international students to convey the message that they are part of, literally, a world-saving movement."

—**Robert Gould,** *Director,*
Conflict Resolution,
Portland State University

*To all the messengers bringing
peace to Africa and the world*

Sankofa
Return and get it
This Adinkra symbol represents the importance of learning
from the past and carrying that wisdom into the future.

Messengers of Peace

Inspiring Stories of Africans Creating Peace

DeEtte Beghtol Waleed

Table of Contents

Acknowledgements

Many people inspired this book, beginning with all the students at Mindolo Ecumenical Foundation and Meheba Refugee Settlement in Zambia who taught me more about myself and about Africa than I taught them.

Quentin Kanyatsi and Jose Noé taught me to listen to refugees. Selline Korir showed me the power of women banding together to change their own communities. Eddie Bulongo opened my eyes to the deep and painful realities of ethnic conflicts and child soldiers. Issa Ebombolo taught me the importance of healing our wounds before we can build peace. Issa, Odila Madiamba, Jean Kabengele Tshibanda and other members of Meheba Messengers of Peace showed us that determination and perseverance are more important to an organization than UN funding.

The General Board of Global Missions of the United Methodist Church has graciously allowed me to use their graphic "Just Peace" for the cover of the book.

I am greatly indebted to Kassy Daggett for her excellent skills in graphic arts and for putting it all together; to Victor Rozek for his very skillful editing, and to Jāla for making it possible. My writing group: Esther Elizabeth, Mia Nyschens, Judith Bradshaw, Kassy Daggett, Jackleen de la Harpe, and Melissa Bennett, taught me to take myself seriously as a writer. And I could not write at all without the support of Jāla, assisted by Ruby and Gracie.

Foreword

I went to Zambia to teach. I had no idea how much I would learn.

I was sent to Zambia in 2000 by the Mennonite Central Committee where I coordinated the Peacebuilding and Conflict Transformation program at Mindolo Ecumenical Foundation, a small community college in Kitwe. Shortly after I arrived, I met Olubanke King Akerele, then Coordinator of UN Programs for Zambia. Together we created the Messengers of Peace program.

Messengers of Peace started as a workshop to help ordinary people from community organizations learn peacebuilding skills. We gathered together Christian, Muslim and Baha'i women from Zambia and their neighbors in Congo. Women and men came from many sectors of the community to learn peace together. Ms. King Akerele was so committed to the project that she funded it with her personal discretionary funds.

We also knew that refugees need peacebuilding skills. Refugees understand better than the rest of us how important peacebuilding is, personally as well as internationally. They are eager to learn how to live peacefully. We designed a workshop especially for refugees in Meheba Refugee Settlement, a community of 50,000 refugees mostly from Angola, Congo, Rwanda, and Burundi. UN High Commission for Refugees (UNHCR) in Zambia saw the importance of the program and funded the training. The UNHCR was so pleased with the results that they wanted us to replicate it in the other seven refugee camps in Zambia.

We quickly learned that the refugees themselves were the best teachers for other refugees. They understood the needs and challenges of refugees much better than a white North American. So we trained a group of 20 refugees and sent them out to the far reaches of Zambia to meet their compatriots. We insisted that each training team be comprised of equal numbers of men and women. Levels of formal education were not as important as the trainers' compassion and ability to relate to the trauma of refugees.

The refugee trainers taught us an important lesson: Refugees need to deal with their own trauma before they can begin to make peace with others. At the suggestion of our refugee trainers we began the training with trauma healing sensitization. The results were amazing. Talking to a sensitive listener about the trauma of being a refugee is in itself an act of healing and peacebuilding. We heard stories of families being uprooted from home, leading children through minefields, encountering warring forces who tried to kidnap anyone big enough to hold a gun, and others too gruesome to repeat.

* * *

We hear many tragedies from Africa. What our sorrowing world needs is stories of hope, courage, compassion, self sacrifice, and love. I hope you enjoy meeting a few of my African friends in these pages. They exemplify those values.

Peace to you on your journey,
DeEtte Beghtol Waleed

Introduction

These stories introduce you to the true heroes of Africa. They are just a few of the many stories I experienced and heard from the Messengers of Peace. If you want more details about the Messengers of Peace program, flip quickly to the last chapter. If you want your heart to be broken open by amazing tales of everyday courage and compassion, read all the stories in-between.

These stories are all based on real people and real situations. I met each protagonist personally and have walked with many of them on their peacebuilding journeys.

Zuze came to the refugee camp as a teenager and now heads a family with teenage children still confined to "a prison without walls" which is the refugee camp. He agonizes at the thought of more generations of his family remaining separated from their homeland. Yet he turns his frustration into leadership, teaching students of many ages how to resolve conflicts.

The story of **Selline** takes us to Kenya and details the struggle of brave women to change traditional practices of Female Genital Mutilation (FGM). Selline and networks of women's groups rescue fleeing "FGM refugees," working to reconcile families, replacing repressive practices with healthy initiation rituals.

Leon is a courageous Congolese government official who risked his life to escape from an oppressive regime. He and his family left a life of luxury and privilege to live in a snake-infested grain warehouse in a refugee camp because his conscience would no longer let him serve an unjust leader.

Novas is a child in Zambia. African children, like novas in the night sky, go from being hardly visible to amazing us with their brightness. According to Fr. Charley Thomas, an Anglican Bishop in Zambia,

> "Traditionally, people in Africa (Zambia, Tanzania) didn't worry about who children belonged to. They belonged to the village. It didn't matter who the father was. It was only the coming of Western religion that made them start to appear to care for nuclear families."

Novas gets caught up in the collision of those cultural expectations and the AIDS epidemic.

In the same way **Eddie** finds himself entangled in ethnic clashes between Tutsis and Hutus that stretch far beyond national borders. A Congolese young man who flees the civil war in his country finds himself the enemy in a refugee camp because he is half-Tutsi and half-Hutu. He learns that fighting back doesn't solve the problem but peacebuilding does.

Françoise is an attractive young woman caught up in ethnic conflicts within her own country, as well as changing gender expectations. She finds surprising allies and unexpected strategies for making peace in her city.

A Muslim man in an overwhelmingly Christian refugee camp, **Issa** overcomes personal struggles to build peace in his settlement and nationwide. He uses the lessons he learns from his ordeal to teach others to resolve conflicts.

Patience, a young Zambian woman who has seen the world outside her home village, struggles with emerging roles for women in her country. Her strife spreads as she becomes one of millions of young African women who find themselves widowed by the AIDS epidemic.

The final chapter gives a glimpse of how **Messengers of Peace** was born and developed in communities and refugee camps in Zambia. It describes the pioneering path that is still followed by the Meheba Messengers of Peace, a non-profit organization developed and sustained by the refugees of Meheba Refugee Settlement.

Each story provides a model for grassroots peacebuilding from the personal to the international. I hope you, dear reader, can find your own path to peace and share it in your world.

Messengers of Peace

Akono Nau

The leg of a hen

The hen treads on her chicks but she does not kill them.
This is a symbol of the ideal nature of parents,
both protective and corrective.

Chapter 1

Zuze

I walk the long dusty path from the secondary school where I teach to my home. I walk past three kilometers of dry fields where other refugees grew sweet potatoes last season, past abandoned fields where my neighbors have given up all hope of making a living. The holes in my shoes let in the soft dust of the path. I can't take off my shoes, as my students do when they walk home. A teacher must be more dignified than that.

On the small rise behind me sits the school, six cement-brick classrooms with corrugated tin roofs, Meheba Refugee Settlement Secondary School. Each classroom has an old rough blackboard and sometimes enough desks for all the students to sit down. The students stay at their desks in their classroom, and teachers come in and out according to the schedule. There are no books. Students have to write the lessons in notebooks they bring from home. I have to bring my own chalk and eraser. At the beginning of the year there was enough chalk to write on the board. Now, at the end of the year, my preciously hoarded supply of chalk is long gone.

My office is a small closet I share with Mr. Bwembya, the science teacher. Beside the school is a grassy area where students play soccer after school. Sometimes they play with a real soccer ball. More often they make do with a bunch of plastic bags rolled up together.

My wife Elizabeth is waiting for me, as she does every day after school, at the gate that keeps the chickens out of our small garden. Our house matches the school, cement block walls, tin roof. Because I'm a teacher we get a better house than our neighbors. Most of them had to build their own houses from mud bricks, like my parents did when they first came here.

My parents brought me to this refugee camp from Angola when I was 13. They wanted to find a place where their children could grow up without bombs falling around them. They brought us to this settlement, hundreds of square kilometers of open grasslands far from familiar rivers and hills. They didn't imagine their grandchildren would still be here.

My parents lived and died here. I found an Angolan refugee to marry, and our children are now repeating our pattern. But this is not Angola. This is Zambia, hundreds of kilometers from Angola. Separated from Angola by borders with armed guards. I'm not Zambian. Zambia only allows me to live here because the UN has made refugees an economic import. Zambians only tolerate me if I stay in the camp and remember my place. I am an outsider, a foreigner. I am not home. But where is home? The place where I was born, where my umbilical cord is buried, is now a foreign land to me. It's a land still torn apart by war, even though the shooting has now stopped. Do I belong there? In a land I barely remember? I don't feel like I belong in Zambia. Is my homeland this refugee camp? Do I have a home?

Anna, my oldest daughter entered secondary school this year, so we often walk to and from school together. Anna is as beautiful as her mother. And she's smart. She scored the highest in her class on the seventh-grade exams. Today she is staying late to study for her end-of-the-year exams. I welcome the solitude of walking home alone. Walking home gives me time to relax a bit, time to think about something besides the drudgery of teaching. I can mull over my future. I need to make a major decision for my family.

When the civil war officially ended last year, the UN High Commission for Refugees began making plans for all Angolans to return home. They have been holding meetings to push us toward repatriation. They don't tell us we have a choice. Just that we will be going. Last month five buses left the camp crammed with families, all their belongings stacked on the roofs. They packed up years of their lives to go back to Angola.

The first ones were eager to go back. But already I've heard rumors that the buses stopped at the first border town. People said all the roads were destroyed by the war. There are no bridges left to cross the rivers. Refugees were told their fields are filled with other families or with land mines. So a hundred families are now stranded without food or any way to go forward or back. Is that going home?

But if I decide to stay in Zambia, I can't become a Zambian. Even though the UN Convention on the Rights of Refugees says I have a right to change my citizenship, Zambia says "no." None of my six children are Zambian citizens, even though they were born in Zambia. But neither are they Angolans. We are citizens of no-man's-land. Where are the borders of our homeland? Should I move my family to a land none of us knows? Should we stay in Zambia where we are foreigners?

So I walk. One step at a time.

Everyone walks. All the students and teachers walk to school. There is no bus to take anyone to school here, actually no buses at all inside the refugee settlement. And, of course, no teachers have the luxury of cars. The Zambia Department of Education barely pays us enough to feed our families. UN workers have cars and drivers. Jesuit Refugee Service has a few cars for their staff. The only other vehicles we see in this whole settlement are the trucks that come in to haul the sweet potatoes at harvest time. The rest of us are lucky if we have a bicycle.

One day when it was raining hard after school, a UN driver picked me up and gave me a ride as far as the junction. But that was only because I'm a teacher and he knows me, and he had already dropped off the UN official he was driving to a meeting. UN drivers are not allowed to pick up refugees. UN High Commission for Refugees says their drivers aren't a taxi service for us. I understand. If people see a driver pick me up, tomorrow there will be a line of hundreds of others waiting to be picked up as well. There are 50,000 refugees here, many muddy roads, and only a few UN drivers.

So I walk.

My father was proud when I became a teacher. He told me that in our traditions teachers are given great respect. They are the guardians of culture, the ones who pass on the important lessons from our ancestors to the young. I don't feel like a respected custodian of traditions. In a refugee camp the old beliefs are lost in the fight for survival. There are no chiefs to lead ceremonies to teach our children our ways. The few elders who are here are isolated and frustrated. Teenagers are more interested in alcohol and cell phones than in learning traditions and legends.

So I walk.

A couple of months ago there was a serious fight between two of my students. The boys are always ready to fight as we get closer to the end of the school year. As usual it was a Congolese boy fighting with an Angolan boy. I understand. I know their passion to prove themselves men. I've spent longer than they have dealing with the frustrations of a refugee camp. I recognize better than they do how it feels to be caged up with no escape. Their fathers, pressed down by the weight of disappointment, have been encouraging their sons to become the warriors they never were, ready to get revenge for past generations' battles with their ancient enemies. But schools and governments tell the students to keep it all stuffed inside. Keep locked up your father's inner wars as well as your own. It's no surprise that their bottled up anger explodes.

This fight was more serious than usual. The headmaster took the Congolese boy to the hospital. I try to think of ways to teach students better ways of dealing with their frustrations. The day after the fight I heard about the Messengers of Peace training. People from a college were coming to teach refugees how to deal with problems in the camp. They were also going to prepare us Angolans for repatriation. I saw a spark of hope. I told the headmaster I wanted to take the training so I could stop some of the student fights. He didn't want to let me take the days off. It's hard to find someone to take over my classes. But he allowed me to go.

We're just beginning the Messengers of Peace training. From the first day we started to deal with the rivalries between Congolese and Angolans. There are people of both nationalities in the training. When the trainers asked us to identify conflicts in the camp, those rivalries were the first that came up. The trainers put us in groups and asked us to talk about what we liked and what we didn't like about the other group. I could see that was exactly what my students needed, ways to talk out their differences.

I asked some of the other Messengers of Peace to help me work with the boys at my school. We're taking it on as our project. We need to start training the next generation of boys how to be warriors in a healthy way. We all need to find a manhood that can be strong without fists. If we don't give them a better way to show they are tough, our countries will always be at war. We will be creating still more generations of refugees.

Elizabeth

I stand beside our gate looking up the path for my husband Zuze to come home from school. Every day I look forward to seeing him appear around the last bend in the path. He is my husband, and also my friend. Our marriage was arranged by our parents, as all marriages were in our generation, but I loved him from the first time I saw him and I love him still after 16 years of marriage.

Zuze is a good man. He doesn't beat me like many of my friends' husbands do. Too many women believe that all men beat their wives. Some men start beating their fiancées even before they are married. I can't understand why any woman would consent to marry a man if he beat her. I can't understand any parents who would force a daughter to marry a man, or to stay with him, if he beats her. I guess the girls think they don't have many choices in a refugee camp. But I teach my daughters they will be better off single for life than forever tied to a man who doesn't respect them. My friends think I'm stupid to teach my daughters such things. They think if my daughters have such attitudes they won't be able to find husbands. I say, "My daughters have brains and hearts as good as any man. God created women to be men's helpers. The only thing they learn from beatings is how to duck."

I also teach my daughters that they don't need to have as many children as I did. I love each and every one of my children, but in this day and age we don't need to follow our mothers' advice to have lots of children. Paying for school fees for daughters and sons is too difficult if you have so many. And with better maternity care more of our children survive. The men who insist that their wives have many children are more concerned about their own puffed-up images than they are about the health of their wives and children.

I lean on my hoe to ease the pain in my back. It's hard work raising enough vegetables and chickens to feed our eight stomachs. Especially in Zambia's arid soil. My mother always used to say Angola's fields were the best in the world, and those here could never compare. She probably was just longing for the home and garden she lost when they fled the war. Home always seems best. But I make the best of my life. It doesn't do me any good to cry over what I can't have. I have my husband and my children, all of them alive and well. What more could a woman want?

My two youngest children, Thomas and Alicia, are playing in the dusty path beside our house. But they keep their eyes open to spy their daddy coming around the corner. Their older brothers make cars out of bottle caps and wire for Thomas. And Alicia carefully balances the doll I made from scraps of cloth on her back and wraps her securely in a *chitenge* cloth. She carries her doll on her back the same way I carried her and all her brothers and sisters until they were old enough to walk. That way the babies are closest to their mother's hearts. The babies are safe and content while mothers get their work done.

Our four older children are inside working on their homework. No matter how much they complain, I don't let them come outside until their homework is finished. With their father being a teacher and all, they musn't shame us by getting bad grades. I know how important it is for them to pass their exams and get into secondary school. We'll try to send them all to college, even the girls, at least to teachers' college or business college. In these times, girls need to be able to earn their own living. It's foolish to count on a husband to support them all their lives. Not every woman can be as lucky as I am.

Thomas seems to be doing OK. He's recovered from the scare we had a few weeks ago. He had malaria, as we all do from time to time, but then his fever got really high. I wrapped him in a blanket and ran to the camp administrator's office to get a pass to take him to the hospital outside the camp. Mr. Mwamba was not in his office, and his secretary didn't know when he would be back. I was really frantic. He's the only one who can sign a pass to get me out of the camp. The only hospital is 26 kilometers away in Solwezi. The bus only runs twice a day, so I knew I had to be there to catch the second bus. I ran to the main gate with Thomas, but I didn't know if the bus driver would let me on the bus. He isn't supposed to let me on without a pass. He could see I had a sick child. I wasn't just trying to lie to get out of the camp. I sat on the ground with Thomas trying to keep his fever down with wet cloths.

We just waited until the bus was almost full. The driver doesn't leave until the bus has as many passengers as can squeeze in. Everyone could see how sick Thomas was, but the driver didn't want to get into trouble for letting us on without a pass. I didn't know whether to offer him a bribe or not. I didn't have but a few *kwacha* and I didn't know if he would be insulted that I offered such a small bribe or if he would just take pity on us and squeeze us in at the last minute.

Finally the driver was tired of waiting for one more passenger to fill the bus. He nodded his head at me to get on the bus. I have never been so grateful. Some of the other refugee women thanked the driver for his kindness. I got Thomas to the hospital and the nurses gave him some quinine. I was worried the whole time that some UN people would see us in town and ask for our passes. But we made it back home safely. What a relief.

Anna

My father Zuze is a good guy. I get teased a lot by the kids in my classes because my father is one of our teachers. It's not cool to be a teacher's kid. But I know they respect him. This year I'm in second-ary school where he teaches. Sometimes we walk home from school together and he talks to me like I'm a grown-up. I'm proud of him. He treats all the kids with respect. He teaches *maths*, but he also talks with kids about being a refugee and about peace.

It's really strange. Everybody here is a refugee. Everybody feels like they don't belong here. But no one talks about it. It's like the world outside the refugee camp controls everything we do, but there is an invisible wall between us and them.

There are a few kids in our school who are boarding students. They aren't refugees but they applied to our school because it's easier to get a place than in other secondary schools in Zambia. So those kids have to decide if they want to go to school in the middle of nowhere or not get into any school. What a choice! The rest of us don't have a choice. Only one school on this side of the fence.

We learn about the rest of the world from those boarding students. Things like surfing the internet in internet cafés. Like rich kids having their own cell phones. Cool things like that. We're stuck on our own planet with only each other to talk to.

Boys in our school fight a lot. Some boys argue and yell at each other about stealing someone's girlfriend. They think girls like them to be tough. They don't know that the girls think fighting is stupid.

The bloodiest fights happen between Congolese guys and Angolans. Last week it was Jean Paul, a Congolese. We were all just sitting on the grass eating our lunches when he strutted by. He stuck out his chest and rolled up his sleeves to show off his muscles. He was acting just like the rooster in our yard. It was hard not to laugh. Then he said something under his breath. I didn't even hear what he said. But my cousin Matthew, an Angolan like me, just exploded. Matthew has always had a hot temper. If he wasn't my cousin, I'd say he was a jerk. I think he was just waiting for his chance to beat up Jean Paul. All the boys started yelling and encouraging them. They had their fists up and ready to go at it when my dad came and broke it up. He got them to sit down and talk about fighting and how it doesn't solve anything. Since he started the Messengers of Peace training, he does the same thing with my brothers when they argue at home.

Dad told me later the other Messengers of Peace have been helping people in the camp when they have problems with each other. I think he even went next door when he heard our neighbor start beating his wife. I didn't pay any attention because it happens so often. But the slapping sounds stopped as soon as my father knocked on their door. I saw my mother smile at him when he came back. She's glad he's a Messenger of Peace. She told me we'll have to stretch the food portions for a while because Dad has to take time off for the trainings and doesn't get paid for it. But she says it's worth it.

The other day on our walk home from school I told Dad about a problem among the girls. In most families girls take a back seat to the boys. Fathers send their children to school, but when money is tight, it's the girls who have to drop out. Some fathers say it's not worth it to send girls to school at all. The only thing girls are good for is money in a father's pocket when he gets a bride price.

So when a rich guy comes along, girls see a way to get some money to stay in school. It doesn't matter if he's as old as their father and so fat he can hardly breathe, if he flashes his money around, they start talking about being in love. I remind them they've seen other girls get pregnant and get dumped. But they say, "Oh no. This one is different. He really loves me." Puh-leeze!

So Dad and I were talking about it on our way home from school, and he said, "What do you think we can do about it?"

It popped into my head that girls need other girls to support them. Their mothers go along with their fathers because they're afraid to speak up. But if girls have support from other girls to resist the sugar-daddies, they can stay strong together. Dad told me the Messengers of Peace are trying to decide which conflicts in the camp are the most urgent. He convinced the others that we need a girls club in our school, a Keep-Strong club, and they got the headmaster to approve it.

So now our club meets every Tuesday during lunch. We talk about all kinds of problems girls have. Mostly we encourage each other to stay in school. My Dad is the advisor to the club, but he doesn't come to the meetings unless we ask him. The girls like it that he lets us learn leadership skills and doesn't tell us what to do all the time. At the first meeting of the club he told us the Messengers of Peace would do whatever they could to support girls, especially to help us resist sugar-daddies. At first only a few girls came to the meetings, but we're spreading the word and inviting our friends. Dad asked the Messengers of Peace to see if they can find money to buy us T-shirts that say Keep Strong Club on the front and Messengers of Peace on the back. That would be way cool.

Zuze and his family chose to remain in Zambia. They will remain in Meheba Refugee Settlement until Zuze finds a teaching position in another school.

Bin Nka Bi
No one should bite the other.
This symbol cautions against provocation and strife.

Chapter 2

Selline

When her office phone rang that morning Selline Korir was not prepared for the news. She had worked for the National Council of Churches of Kenya for five years. Her office near her home in Eldoret, Kenya was often a center of activity for issues concerning women. But this emergency eclipsed them all.

> The quavering voice of Pastor Gitobu on the other end of the line said, "Selline, I need your help. Last night three young girls knocked on my door asking for a place to sleep. All three ran away from their homes in the villages. They were about to be taken to the bush to be cut, and they refused to go."

> "God save us!" replied Selline, falling back in her chair. "Bless you, pastor. Thank you so much for taking them in."

Selline couldn't suppress her body's shudder in horror at the mention of female genital mutilation (FGM). She had been fighting this barbaric practice since she was a child, herself threatened with the procedure. Girls between the ages of 6 and 12 are taken to remote rural locations in the dead of night. Women of the village hold down her arms and legs while an old woman with a dull knife or a rusty razor blade cuts off the child's clitoris and labia. In the most severe forms the remaining genital tissue is sewn together to make a smooth surface leaving only a match-stick-sized hole for urine and menstrual blood to pass through. The girl's legs are tied together to stop the bleeding. She is kept with a group of other "cut" girls for a few days while village women give the girls instruction on how to be a proper traditional woman.

Selline remembered her own experience, more than fifteen years before, when her parents had sent her away to school in India in order to avoid her ethnic group's traditional "cutting." With her college degree in hand, she had returned to Kenya determined to help women overcome the many cultural practices which are physically and emotionally destructive to women.

Then her mind returned to Pastor Gitobu on the other end of the line. "I'll phone the women this morning. We'll meet as soon as we can to figure out what to do. I'll get back to you by this afternoon."

"Thank you. The girls are safe for now. We have enough millet to feed us for a few days. You know I'll do all I can in order to save other girls from the fate my late sister endured," the pastor replied.

"I know, Pastor. May her soul rest in peace. I'll see who can meet this morning to work out a plan."

The first phone call Selline made was to her husband. Paul, an

Anglican priest had supported her work with the women for more than four years, since they met at the the National Council of Churches of Kenya. His work in conflict resolution complimented her work with the women. She needed his assurance and prayer before she tackled this difficult situation. Then she could move on to calling the network of women who formed the Rural Women's Peace Link. She was sure some of the women would be available, even at this short notice, to meet with Pastor Gitobu.

Mary was the next one Selline called that morning. "Come quickly. There are girls who have run away from being cut. We need to find safe places for them to stay."

Oh yes, of course. I'll call the others. I'll get as many as we can and meet you at your office."

As they trickled in by twos and threes to Selline's office that morning, the women of Rural Women's Peace Link were filled with a mixture of emotions. They wanted the girls to be safe, but they also knew the pain of the families left behind. Each of the women had stories of how she, her sisters, her mother, her grandmothers, generations back as far as anyone remembered, had suffered the cutting. Each had stories of sisters who hadn't survived, those who had bled to death in the desert, or those who had lived but suffered infections for the rest of their lives because of the cutting. But some women still clung to tradition, no matter how painful. Now the women of Rural Women's Peace Link were being challenged to protect the daughters of the next generation. Seven women met with Selline and Mary that morning to come up with a plan. They gathered food and emergency supplies. Pastor Gitobu agreed to let the girls stay in his home. But more girls arrived the next night and the next.

Selline was not prepared for the waves of girls who somehow found out about the FGM refuge safe house. "So many, Lord. We're up to thirty-two girls and more arriving every day." Word spread fast on the streets of Eldoret. It was like fire spreading through the underbrush. Girls sneaked out of windows in the middle of the night and raced across the desert and down mountains to get to Eldoret. Each hoped there was safety and protection in the city. Word was whispered from one girl to the next and they found the pastor's house. Each one was more surprised than the last to see the crowd of girls filling the house and spilling over into the church.

The women began meeting weekly to map out strategy.

> Mary dealt with practical issues, "We're running out of floor space for the girls to sleep in Pastor Gitobu's church. Can some of us squeeze a girl or two into our houses?" Several hands went up.

> "Most of the girls don't even have a change of clothes and the rainy season will start any day now," Priscilla added. "Can someone go with them to the market to buy shoes and some cloth to use as skirts?" A couple of hands went up.

> "Remember, don't go out with more than two or three girls at a time. We don't want to attract attention," Rebecca added. "Their parents are looking for them to force them back home." Heads nodded.

Others in the rural women's network were supportive, helping to find safe homes, blankets, clothes, food, and other necessities to help the Eldoret women keep up with the tide of girls seeking refuge.

> "We need to start planning now for the long term. Where will they go to school?"

"I'm contacting boarding schools to find places for as many as we can." Selline offered, checking her lists. "As of now we have three headmistresses who have been very helpful. They're holding spaces open as long as we assure them that we'll find at least part of the tuition money. I'm waiting for responses from some others. I was surprised to find so many headmistresses also working to end FGM. They tell me our girls are courageous role models for the other girls in their schools. So they'll do everything they can to squeeze them in."

"But where will we find the money?" Priscilla asked with a frown. "It'll take – O Lord, I can't imagine! – thousands of shillings for their tuition."

"God provides." Selline responded with a pat to Priscilla's arm. "I'm writing emails and making phone calls to international women's groups and foundations. I'm pulling in all the contacts I can find. People are eager to help once they know what we're doing. But I could still use more help on this. Can someone help me make phone calls?" Brenda raised her hand.

But Selline's confidence sometimes melted after the women left her office. Could she really find all the boarding schools she needed to keep the girls safe? Would the money arrive in time to pay for uniforms and books? At home in the evenings she collapsed, letting the huge responsibility she had undertaken wash over her. Paul often found her slumped in a chair, her cup of tea grown cold, the baby asleep in his crib, dinner the farthest thing from her mind. He asked his young, unmarried sister to come and stay with them to help Selline with the household.

In moments when she felt overwhelmed, Selline took walks, and often found herself at Pastor Gitobu's church. She always found a cluster of girls eager to weave stories into their cooking or chatting. She told them the story of her own journey out of the village and away from the cutting. Stories of other women's survival. Stories of women who followed, yet changed, the traditional culture, sustained by women yearning to make a better world for girls.

The women kept meeting, drawing strength from each other.

"We have another urgent problem," said Selline. "I'm getting calls from parents who have heard their daughters are here. They're demanding that I tell them where to find their girls. They feel embarrassed in their villages because their daughters aren't following traditions. Some really believe they will remain physically children forever if they aren't cut".

"It's amazing that people believe those old myths," cried Pauline.

"Yes, we all know traditional ways change very slowly," answered Mary. "All of the parents fear that their daughters won't find husbands. They don't want the burden of supporting the girls for the rest of their lives."

"Old ways die hard," moaned Rebecca.

"Change is hard for all of us," Selline replied soothingly. "We have to help them see how change benefits them. I'm setting up meetings with parents and grandparents to help everyone understand more."

Mary sounded alarmed. "Are the girls ready to meet their parents?"

"Some are." Selline responded patting Mary's arm. "It's my job to make sure the meetings are safe. Each girl can choose for herself if she wants to attend the meeting. I let the girls know that I won't allow any girl to return home unless she's ready. The parents respect my authority in the community, especially since I'm married to a priest. I'll tell them my own story about how my parents protected me. They'll relax a bit when they hear that I've never been cut and still I'm married, I have a child and I'm respected."

Selline carefully listened to parents and daughters. She respected the views of both sides even when her heart was on the side of the girls. The meetings seemed to calm things down. Parents were less hostile when they could see that their daughters were OK, even though most girls still refused to return to their villages. After the first meetings, girls who were afraid to meet with their parents began to build trust. Selline returned to her office after each meeting exhausted but hopeful.

Selline also used the meetings to educate parents. She asked Paul to accompany her to help the fathers see things differently. He told them, "God values our bodies. God made our bodies beautiful and perfect as they are. Cutting off parts damages what our Creator made. We need to teach our daughters to be proud of their bodies and to protect them from anyone misusing them." Paul's bold words amazed the parents. They were astounded that a man, especially a priest, would speak about "women's matters."

Selline told the parents stories about women in remote villages who could not safely give birth because the opening for the child to emerge had been sewn together so tightly after the cutting. They had heard whispered rumors of such things but didn't want to believe them. She confirmed, "The birth process literally tore their bodies apart and their husbands threw them out as useless. I know you want healthy daughters and to have them accepted in your villages. We need to work together to make a plan that helps all of us."

After some months the list of boarding schools was long enough to match the list of the FGM refugees. Women from the networks, loaded with bundles of supplies, boarded buses to accompany each girl to school. Each girl was carefully handed into the arms of a head teacher or dormitory matron who knew the importance of protecting her from parents' kidnapping. Whenever possible each girl had a substitute auntie near the school who she could contact for support. Girls began to relax into school routines, under the ever-vigilant eyes of headmistresses. The networks of rural women raised funds for uniforms, books, and toiletries, because they all agreed that girls' education was important. But at the same time, the groups struggled with whether they should be supporting girls who were rebelling against their parents.

During her years of work for women, Selline had developed contacts in Europe, America and Asia. Her friends responded to her passionate pleas. She found foundations working for women's rights and kept on telling the saga of the FGM refugees. Like the story of Moses and manna in the desert, somehow there was always enough to meet the need.

The women's networks also began educational meetings in the villages. Women from each village tackled the issues that were the most difficult for their hometowns. Women discovered they had the power to change long-held myths. They devised healthy initiation rituals to replace the harmful ones. They openly discussed the dangers and helped people search for alternatives. People responded in creative ways.

The story is not ended. Some of the girls who found Pastor Gitobu's open door chose to remain in cites, setting aside their yearning to return to their homes. Some decided to return, knowing the knife awaited them the following year. Some clung to the shelter of their new network of aunties, struggling to stand with one foot in their villages and the other on the shaky ground of change. These courageous young women, no longer the frightened girls who escaped to Pastor Gitobu's sanctuary, are telling their stories to sisters and cousins. And their stories are changing the world.

Denkyem
crocodile
The crocodile lives in the water yet breathes the air.
This symbol demonstrates an ability to
adapt to circumstances.

Chapter 3

Leon

It's evening. In Zambia the light changes from bright sunlight to inky blackness in a matter of minutes. Far from any city, the paths of the refugee camp are lit only by the moon and the flickering light of candles and kerosene lamps filtering through neighbors' windows. Leon waits outside the large metal grain warehouse as his wife, Charity, beds down their two young children on mattresses on the dirt floor inside. She leaves the three older children to finish their homework in the dim light of kerosene lamps.

Charity steps out, softly closing the metal door so she won't disturb the children. The couple has a few stolen moments of quiet together at the end of the day to shake off the dreary dust of the refugee camp and enjoy the cool night air. Tall and lean, his nappy hair shaved to his smooth skull, Leon takes the hand of his pudgy wife. Refugee rations have not yet reduced Charity's girth, built on years of Belgian chocolates and the African belief that a fat wife is the sign of a wealthy man. Life in a windowless metal grain warehouse, without running water or electricity, is not what either of them expected three months ago in Congo.

Then, as mayor of the southern region, appointed by President Laurent Kabila himself, Leon enjoyed an office with elaborate mahogany furniture. He smiles every time he remembers the thick red carpet leading up the circular stairway to his office. Only he was allowed to walk on that red carpet. Even important visitors from America were strictly instructed to walk only on the sides of the stairs. Definitely not on the red carpet. He enjoyed the servants provided for him by the government. He tried to be fair and generous to the many people who waited on him at home and at his office. He could afford to reward their loyalty with handsome gifts on national holidays and at Christmas. Charity could have as many dresses as she liked decorated with traditional ornate embroidery. She could change her hairstyle every week, from one wig to the next, or spend hours with three personal hairdressers who braided orange or red ribbons into her hair. She could dress her children in the latest styles from France or South Africa. She could furnish her house in the most elaborate style she wished. She never looked at a price tag.

Now in the refugee camp, luxury is the one ripe mango the children brought back from their exploration of the camp. Meheba Refugee Settlement is now home. Two hundred and eighty square miles of dirt, separated into zones A through F by a few roads, deep mud for six months of the rainy season and blowing dust the rest of the year.

Instead of a house with many windows looking out over wide verandas, now they live in a windowless grain warehouse. Instead of tiers of guards carefully checking the IDs of all visitors before they were allowed up the long tree-lined driveway, they now have one guard at night. His job is to guard the supply of corn for 50,000 refugees, and only incidentally Leon and his family. Leon and Charity have the privilege of a guard. The other refugees provide whatever security they can with a machete beside an unlockable door. Leon has a guard because he still knows too much about Congo President Laurent Kabila. This close to the Congo border it would be easy for someone to slip inside the camp and drive a knife into his chest. The guard keeps out intruders. He doesn't keep out the snakes who come to feast on rats in the sacks of corn.

Yes, Leon reflects, life was good in Congo. As a talented young man he had quickly moved through the intricate maze of government bureaucrats. Making important friends here, impressing the right people there. At 40 he had reached what some considered the height of a political career. Mobutu, the all-powerful dictator who built himself gold and glass palaces all over the country, had appointed him mayor of Likasi, then promoted him to be mayor of the southern region. When Laurent Kabila overthrew Mobutu and declared himself President of the Democratic Republic of Congo, Leon held onto his mayor's robes. He believed Kabila's promises. Leon was ready to see some of the country's wealth trickle down to the people. He believed Kabila would create a government that brought the justice the people had craved for decades. He thought finally the government would serve the people.

But Kabila never took off his general's uniform when he became President. He surrounded himself with other generals and expected the same unquestioning loyalty from his mayors. The promises of change soon became buried in deep piles of official directives. Leon tentatively asked questions: "What is the purpose of this order?" and "Didn't the President promise things would change?" Scowls of warning were the only answer. Leon remembered the promises. He knew about the skeletons in the closets.

When Leon's questions became more pointed, soldiers arrived at his home late one evening and took him to a jail he didn't know existed. He was released only after he paid his captors 5,000 U.S. dollars. They were not interested in Congolese francs.

Leon sought advice from trusted friends, businessmen, people outside the government. They told him, "Lay low. Quit stirring up trouble." Leon's conscience wrestled with his privilege. If he shut his mouth, he could continue to enjoy his nice job with all its benefits.

After the third arrest, and the third payment of thousands of U.S. dollars, a friend whispered to Leon, "It appears you're not getting the message. The next time it will not be handcuffs, but a bullet."

Leon wasn't sure how to tell Charity about this new threat. He certainly couldn't make it a topic of family dinner conversation around their massive mahogany dining table beneath the European crystal chandelier. Who knew if the servants were reporting their every word to their enemies? Or if the money from USAID that was called "economic development aid" had paid for electronic bugs vying for space in the woodwork with tropical beetles? But it was clear to him that his policies and opinions were now threatening his survival. Clearly Charity needed to know soon. So after dinner during their stroll on the well-tended lawns, they came up with a plan.

Within a few days Leon withdrew as much cash as he could without raising suspicion. Charity packed family mementos and a few clothes in six small bags. The baby couldn't be expected to carry a suitcase. Neither parent told the children where they were going. They loaded the five children into the car one night after dinner, put a basket of food and water in the trunk, met the children's questions with a finger to their lips, and drove the back roads towards Zambia. It was close to midnight when Leon pulled the car to the side of the road less than a kilometer from the border crossing. They were still out of sight of the small hut where border guards dozed next to the locked gate.

They could finally tell the children where they were going. Even if the car was bugged, they could be across the border before anyone could catch them. All of them regretted leaving their home, their toys. None of them could have imagined what was ahead of them. Certainly they expected more than dirt floors and makeshift furniture made out of bags of grain. But that dark night, in the last car they would be in for several years, Leon told his children that integrity was the one thing he was not willing to leave behind.

As they wound their way through the underbrush, with everything they now owned in their hands, keeping the children as silent as possible, Leon knew that he couldn't even tell his parents where they were. No relatives or close friends could know how to find them, or if they had survived the trip out of Congo. If family knew how to contact them, they might reveal Leon's location under torture. The moment the family left their golden cage, they became a liability to the government of Congo. Next door in Zambia, or anywhere in Africa, it would be easy for Kabila's thugs to hire someone to silence the dissenter.

Like many refugees before them, they found paths through the underbrush that skirted the border guards. Once they were safely across the border, they didn't need to join the queue waiting for the bus to Meheba, the nearest refugee camp. In his briefcase Leon had carefully preserved the phone number of UN High Commission for Refugees in Zambia. As soon as he revealed his identity, the UN realized how important it was to protect him. His knowledge of the government in Congo could help UN peacekeepers protect others. UN channels started buzzing the next morning to plan how to move the family even farther from the Congo. But for the next few months, they were assigned to Meheba Refugee Settlement.

So here they are, Leon and Charity taking an evening stroll across dusty paths instead of well-manicured lawns. Charity sweeps the dirt floors of their warehouse home with a straw broom her servants would have rejected as too primitive for the garage. Instead of private school with the latest French curriculum, the children learn their school lessons in a classroom of 90 students, without books, copying notes into thin notebooks. Leon walks to the camp's administrative offices every day to give himself something to do and to pick up any tiny scrap of news about when they might be resettled in another country. He dares to hope they might be sent to France or the U.S. He will be grateful for anywhere his family will be safe.

Leon contemplates his privileged position, even in a refugee camp. It isn't fair that he should have the relative luxury of a home with metal walls when other refugees live in tents or in mud-wall houses they have built themselves. He can sometimes talk to UN personnel about his situation. Many of his fellow refugees can't even speak the language of the guards at the gate. He realizes he has privilege, but he must protect his family and do all he can to get them into the best situation he can manage. Where is the balance between fairness and the struggle to survive?

Leon misses the challenges of administering government programs. He misses comfortable beds and food flown in from Europe, China, India. He misses keeping abreast of world affairs on internet news services. But most of all he misses reading books on current economic theory, or any books which might keep his mind agile. Often he drops by the office of the camp administrator, Marcella, just to relieve the boredom.

> One day Marcella beckons him inside. "I've been hoping you'd come by. We've just received word that a group of trainers will be coming to Meheba to train people as Messengers of Peace."

> Leon's eyes brighten. "Tell me more."

> "The UN is sponsoring the program to train refugees to resolve conflicts in the camp and to prepare for repatriation. They'll need translators. Your facility with French, English and Swahili will be very useful."

> "I'd be glad to help. How soon will it start?"

> "Next month. We're just beginning to select participants. You know everyone will be fighting for a chance to be included. But I can make sure you're on the list."

"Thank you. I appreciate your thinking of me."

The opportunity to be involved in meaningful work is like water to Leon's thirsty spirit. He becomes Marcella's administrative assistant in charge of organizing the Messengers of Peace training. As part of the training he contacts Zuze, an Angolan refugee who is his son's math teacher at Meheba Secondary School. Leon suggests that they could reduce tension between Congolese and Angolans, traditional rivals across their shared border, by setting up dialogues between the two groups of refugees. The dialogues, led by Leon and Zuze as translators for their groups, become part of the practical work of the Messengers of Peace.

Leon continues to lead the practical work of the Messengers of Peace, identifying sources of conflict and working with Zuze and others to mediate cross cultural conflicts. The UN officials of the settlement are amazed at the decrease in violence. Zambian police officials assigned to the settlement come to rely on the Messengers of Peace as resources to settle disputes before they escalate into violence.

Leon's fondest dream is to return to Congo to begin the work of healing the wounds of ethnic conflict. He recognizes that ethnic rivalries and favoritism are the tinder that has flamed into Congo's violent civil wars. But he also recognizes that Congo will never again be a safe place for him. It will take generations of peacebuilding to free his homeland from hatred and greed. He is comforted knowing that the Messengers of Peace and their work of reconciling refugees is a step towards stopping wars. For himself the best he can hope for is the day when he can finally sit at a desk in a safe country, pick up the phone, punch in the number he will always remember, hear his mother's "Hello" from Congo and say, "I'm alive. I'm safe. It was all worth it."

After 3 years Leon and his family were accepted by the UN High Commission for Refugees (UNHCR) to be resettled in the U.S.

Funtunfunefudenkyemfunefu
Siamese crocodiles
Symbol of democracy and unity
The Siamese crocodiles share one stomach, yet they fight over food.
This symbol is a reminder that
infighting and tribalism is harmful to all
who engage in it.

Chapter 4

Eddie

The first week of our training as Messengers of Peace, even though I was one of the youngest refugees in the group, I joined some of the others to make a skit to present to the rest of the group. We wanted the trainers from the Zambian college and the few UN workers sitting in on the training to see what life was like for us refugees in Meheba Refugee Settlement.

We made the skit funny, but life in Meheba isn't funny. Our skit showed refugees being stopped at the gate and asked for their passes to leave the camp. Of course they didn't have passes. You have to walk for an hour to get to the office of the camp director. He's a Zambian government official, so of course he's not often in his office. His secretary can't tell us where he is or when he'll be back. In the skit the refugees wanting to go into town "accidentally" dropped money on the ground in front of the guards, and hopped on the bus while the guards picked up the bribe.

We showed refugees trying to sell their sweet potatoes to the only trucker allowed inside the camp. The trucker paid them much less than the rate in Solwezi, just a few kilometers down the road. I wanted to show UN workers stealing mattresses and food from warehouses inside the camp. But we decided we'd better not go that far. The refugees laughed and laughed at our skit. Some of the trainers laughed too. I didn't see any UN people laughing.

My name is Eddie Bulongo. I'm 21. I share a small hut in Meheba Refugee Settlement with my friend Odila. Meheba is in Zambia, a few kilometers from Congo, close enough that some refugees sneak out the back way with a couple of goats strapped to their bicycles. In Congo they can trade the goats for another bicycle. The market for bicycles is good in Meheba.

Odila is about my age and also comes from Congo. We're young enough to remember the pretty girls we left behind, and old enough to know we don't want to fight Congo's wars. Our tiny house is in a long row of mud-brick houses. It is one of tens of thousands of houses for Angolans, Congolese, Rwandans and Burundians in 280 square miles of camp a long way from everywhere. We are surrounded by seas of refugees, all eager to be somewhere else, doing something else, anything else than waiting for the wars to end so we can go home again.

Our house has only one room, barely big enough for two mattresses with about half a meter in between to be able to get out the door without walking on the other bed. A charcoal brazier outside the door is our kitchen. We have to haul water from a tap half a kilometer down the road. There are no women in our house, so if we can't get someone to invite us for dinner, we cook for ourselves. Looking for pretty young girls for wives is more interesting than housekeeping.

Both Odila and I got accepted to the Messengers of Peace training.

Trainers from Mindolo Ecumenical Foundation, a college in Kitwe, came to Meheba to lead the training. Odila was looking for something to keep his mind off living in this prison without walls. He thought he might meet girls from other sections of the camp. I was hoping for something more.

During the training Anna, the main trainer from Mindolo, described courses on their home campus. I quickly wrote down exactly what she said. I've been wanting to continue my education for the 2 years I've been here. When the rebels came to my home village, I had only a month left to finish my college course in business. My mother pushed me out the door with a clean shirt and some food in a bundle. "No time to say goodbye. Go, before they come and force you to be a soldier." I didn't think about picking up my school certificates, but now I need them. I need to show the registrar at Mindolo that I graduated from 12th grade. I can't write to my mother to send them. There is no mail in a refugee camp. My home address might not exist. Our village might be a pile of ashes.

I had high hopes when I heard Anna talk about peacebuilding courses at Mindolo. She said they had scholarships available and liked to have refugees in the courses. She said other students need to learn what it's like to be a refugee. I sure agree with that. I picked up the application for the nine-month course in Peacebuilding and Conflict Transformation. Imagine, nine whole months in a student dormitory instead of squeezed into a cramped room next to Odila. A college course in Zambia could be my ticket out.

I stayed up hours into the night with the application and a kerosene lamp on my bed. I borrowed a clean plastic bag from my friend Tongo and carefully wrapped the application in it to protect it from the dust. I made a hiding spot for the application in a box under my bed to protect it from the leaks in the roof. When your house has no door it's hard to keep anything safe. So I was careful not to talk about my plans to anybody but Odila. Other boys might try to steal my application just for spite.

But the application wasn't yet complete when the trainers from Mindolo came back for the second week. I was shy about talking to Anna personally, but I straightened my back and went up to her after class. I told her I had some questions about the application form and asked her to help me.

"Sure," she said. "I'm staying in the camp guest house. Why don't you come after dinner?"

I was still a bit anxious about meeting with her. After all, she's a white woman from America. What does she care about me?

I ran back to my room and pulled the application from its box. I wiped my hands on my pants before I opened the plastic bag to make sure I didn't get it dirty. Then I carefully put it in my backpack, making sure not to wrinkle it. I was too nervous to eat dinner. Anyway, I didn't want to take the time to cook. Being on time to meet Anna was more important than eating. I walked as fast as I could down the long paths until I saw the light from the guest house windows. Then I started to relax. I didn't want to be sweating when I knocked on her door.

Anna came to the door and invited me in. I had never been inside the guest house before. The closest I ever got was the dusty road out-side. The ceilings were higher than any building I had ever been in. It had tiled floors and two soft couches facing each other with a low table in between. I could see the last of her dinner still on the table by the door to the kitchen. I hoped my stomach wouldn't growl when she was talking to me. Through a door to the kitchen I could see a sink and an electric stove. A bit fancier than my house.

Anna gestured for me to sit on one of the couches. Her eyes seemed friendly enough. She said, "What questions do you have?"

"Here." I pointed to the page and passed it to her.
I tried to relax when she took a minute to read the question. I could see little lines in her forehead. "Well this question asks if you're married. You're not are you?"

"No."

"The next question is whether you have children. Do you?"

"No."

"Then the next question asks for the name of your next of kin. We ask that information in case some emergency happens and we need to notify your family. Since you're not married, you could put the name of your mother or father, or your sisters or brothers."

That was the part that I had been dreading. She leaned closer to me. I think she had a hard time hearing me.

My voice was shaking. I said, "I don't know if any of them are alive."

She was quiet for a long time. Then she said, "I'm so sorry."

I knew Anna hadn't been in Africa long. Maybe she didn't know how important families are to us. Maybe she didn't know how desperately lonely it is to be in a refugee camp, surrounded every moment by 50,000 people, sweeping their houses, cooking their dinners, going to the market, playing football, doing all the daily things people do, knowing you are not connected to anyone. How could she know how I feel? That I sometimes feel like sitting down in the middle of the road, not able to move another step.

Then she said, "I guess you could leave it blank or write 'none.'"

None? I couldn't write "none" on the application. That would be admitting that I would never find any of my relatives. I would never know what happened to them. I would never know how many of them the rebels raped, or the soldiers murdered. I would never know how they died. It would be admitting that all of my letters to the Red Cross asking them to find my family would never be answered. It would be giving up hope. I left the space blank.

The next day I gave the application to Anna. She said she would give it to the registrar at Mindolo. She said she hoped I would be admitted to the program. I could see in her eyes that she meant it.

There wasn't space on the application for me to put all the reasons I wanted to be in the peacebuilding program. I could have told them how I ran from home with the sounds of gunfire behind me, how I hid in the bush for days, how I ran out of food and had to steal to eat, how I nearly stepped on a black Mamba snake, one of the deadliest in all of Africa, how I finally made it to the border.

I could have told them how I met a boy near the border. He looked like he was only about 12. The boy told me he had a gun hidden nearby.

I asked, "Aren't you scared?"

The boy said, "No. The rebels gave me the gun and taught me to shoot it. Then they gave me drugs and a group of them took me back to my village. They grabbed my father and held him up in front of me. They told me to shoot him. Shoot my own father! But they told me if I didn't shoot him, they would shoot me. After that it was easy to shoot other people."

I could have told them how it is to be in Meheba and be half-Tutsi and half-Hutu. There aren't any Tutsi in Meheba. When the UN tried to put Tutsi and Hutu people in the same refugee camp, they fought all the time. They brought the tribal wars with them from Rwanda and Burundi. So Tutsi were moved to Maukwaukwa Refugee Camp and Hutu stayed in Meheba. But I couldn't put half of myself in another camp.

One day about a year before the peacebuilding trainers came to Meheba, a group of Hutu men came up to me. They started yelling at me that my uncles had killed their families. I needed to defend my honor like my uncles taught me. I talked back to them. The men beat me so badly I was in the hospital in Solwezi for four days.

When I was ready to be released, a UN worker came to my room to see how I was doing. She asked me if I wanted to be moved to Maukwaukwa. I looked her straight in the eyes and said, "I'm an enemy there too."

When I got the letter admitting me to the course at Mindolo, I had my bags packed in one hour. Odila was jealous that I got to go before him. But I told him, "You'll get your chance too." And he did.

At Mindolo I met Jeanne, a very pretty girl from Kinshasa, the capitol. Imagine! A girl my age who is also from Congo! She's not a refugee. There's no rebel fighting around Kinshasa. It's a long way from the war. We dated during the time she was at Mindolo, and she promised she'd write me after the course. But I got one letter and then nothing. I guess it's hard to plan a future with someone who doesn't even know where home is.

After I finished the course at Mindolo, I started working with the Meheba Messengers of Peace, the group we formed to work on resolving conflicts among the refugees. It was hard because refugees bring with them the old assumptions that a young man can only be a warrior. I wanted to teach them how to set aside their prejudices about ethnic differences. Without that they will never build peace when they go home. But a great surprise changed my life in a hurry.

Because I'm half Tutsi and half Hutu, I can't go back to Congo. I'll always be someone's enemy there too. Of course I had filled out the forms applying for resettlement to another country, but, like all the others, I didn't believe we would ever be resettled. The idea of actually living in America or even Europe was too impossible to be true.

Then I got two letters. The Red Cross gave me a letter from my sister. My sister! She's alive! My hands shook so badly when I opened the letter I could hardly read it. She's living with our mother in Likasi, a town in the south, away from the war. She told me details about other relatives who died in the fighting. It's good to know at least some of my relatives survived, that my family is alive.

The other letter was even more amazing. I've been approved for resettlement in Denmark. I don't know much about Denmark, except they don't speak French or Swahili there and it's very far north. There aren't any maps or encyclopedias in Meheba to read more about it.

The UN gave me a few pages of information, but not much. All I know is that it's a better place than a refugee camp in the middle of nowhere. I'll get a place to live and some money to get by until I can learn enough of their language to find a job. The UN people told me Tongo and her husband are being resettled there too. At least I'll know someone I can talk to in Denmark.

Eddie is living in Denmark with his wife and son. He is developing a program to help heal the wounds between Tutsis and Hutus in Congo and its neighbors.

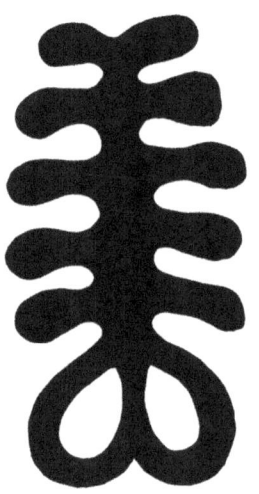

Aya
I am not afraid of you.
I am independent of you.

Chapter 5

Françoise

When work is slow, my boss, Dr. Tshiyenia, and I often discuss our city's political situation. He is Katangese, and therefore given special favors by the government. I'm Kassai and considered lower class. Of course I resent being second class, but it's the way things are in this country and not likely to change. Even though Dr. T and I come from different tribes, he listens to my ideas and we agree quite a lot about ways to improve our city, Likasi, and our country, Congo.

When I applied for this job as a bookkeeper for his veterinary practice, I was surprised that he even looked at my application. I'm an intelligent woman, well trained at our local college, and good looking too, if I do say so myself. Like all good Congolese women I enjoy fixing my hair in the latest styles and wearing beautiful clothes. But good looks don't always get you a job. I almost didn't apply. I thought surely Dr. T would hire one of his own tribe, as businessmen usually do. But he looked at my qualifications and ignored my ethnic heritage.

I'll wager my relatives and Dr. T's relatives would disagree about a lot, maybe even refuse to speak to each other. As the youngest girl in my family, I still live at home with my parents so I hear a lot of the talk that goes on over tea on their front veranda. Lots of grumbling about how badly Kassai are treated by the Katangese, that we are considered greedy, even that we are thieves. My classmates at the college are also very divided along tribal lines. Kassai don't trust Katangese and Katangese sometimes try to lord it over Kassai.

My friends ask me all the time why I'm not married yet. After all, I'm 23, well past the usual marrying age. I just tell them I haven't found the right man yet. That just keeps them lining up endless dates for me. The men are interesting, but I haven't found one that treats me with respect and that would let me keep working after we were married. I'm not ready to give up everything interesting in my world just to be married. I may never be. I don't tell my friends that. They would be shocked.

Our country has been in turmoil for generations. There has always been rivalry and bitterness between the Katangese and the Kassai. I would never shop in the Katangese market. No Kassai woman would expose herself to the humiliation of being turned away by a tomato merchant. But I can hardly blame the Katangese marketeers. Women in the Kassai market act the same. It's the way we have been brought up. We live in separate parts of town. We live separate lives. Most people just accept the way it is.

Then about a year ago all hell broke loose. Pardon my rough language, but it was terrible. The government rounded up all Kassai and forced us to move. Overnight my parents and I had to leave our cozy little one-story house and my mother's garden. Her mother and grandmother before her had tended that garden. We were pulled up like weeds, hundreds of us, and packed into five-story, cold, drafty, cement apartment buildings.

Our whole life was turned upside down. My parents were separated from friends they had known for decades. My brothers and sisters had to find new schools for their children. Since I'm still young and unmarried, I didn't feel the upheaval as much. But it was still a shock. We all had depended on neighbors and local businesses. All of a sudden we were kilometers from all we were used to. No one liked the new arrangements but we were given no other choice.

Then we heard that someone had burned down the Katangese market. We all knew, of course, that it was in retaliation for forcing the Kassai to move. We were astonished that anyone would have the guts to strike back.

A few days later someone burned down our market and set fires in our apartment building. The fires were two floors down from our apartment. We were so used to being in our one-story house, we panicked. We weren't sure how to get out of the building. But my parents were terrified to leave. So they stayed. Looking out the window for hours, watching the smoke from the fires below us. My father said if he had to die, he wanted to die in his own home.

The day after the fires I didn't know whether to talk to Dr. T about it. Yes, we had discussed politics. But maybe this was too much. This was more like war. I was relieved when he brought up the subject.

"Françoise, I heard about the fires. Is your family OK?"

"Yes, thank you for asking. We were scared but unharmed."

"The damage to the markets is terrible."

"Yes. The markets are the way many women support their families. Poor families depend on the few *francs* they earn selling tomatoes and onions. Many people have lost their livelihoods. What good does it do to burn them down?"

"And then to burn people's homes! It's an outrage. The Katangese have brought the wars in the north right into our city. " he said.

I was pleased that he could criticize his own people as well as mine. We agreed that the government should do something to stop the violence.

Then things calmed down a bit. Marketeers from both tribes set up temporary tables again at their old locations. Both sides went back to business as usual. But my family was still stuck living on the 4th floor of a cold cement building.

On the bus I heard people chuckling, "At least *they* are suffering a bit. Maybe now they know how we feel."

"It's always the poor who pay the price."

"You know what they say, 'When the elephants fight, the grass suffers.'"

A few months later Dr. T told me about an economic development workshop that he'd been invited to. It was sponsored by the Anglican diocese for civic leaders in Likasi. It sounded like a very good workshop. I was astounded when he asked if I'd like to come with him. It's pretty unusual for a Congolese businessman to invite any employee to join him at a workshop. But he asked me, a woman, a Kassai woman! He said the organizers were requiring that there be equal numbers of Kassai and Katangese, and equal numbers of women and men at the workshop. Amazing! Miraculous! I phoned my college friends. They just couldn't believe it. They said I was probably going so I could serve him his tea.

The workshop turned out to be even more astounding than I thought. I wasn't expected to serve Dr. T his tea. As a matter of fact there were women there with less education than I have, who are used to kneeling when they serve their husbands. They looked at me when it was time for a tea break. When I served myself tea and sat down again, they did the same. I'll bet it was the first time some of them had ever eaten in the same room with men.

It wasn't the usual three days of boring lectures that half the group snored through in the afternoons. Kanyatsi, the man from Lubumbashi who organized the workshop, didn't let the Katangese dominate the discussions. He even respected the uneducated women. He specifically asked them what they thought. And they had really good ideas. He invited the mayor of Likasi, who is of course Katangese. Our mouths dropped open when he showed up on time. Then after his opening speech, he stayed to listen to what people had to say. He didn't breeze out to his next appointment like he usually does.

A news reporter filmed the whole workshop, not just the speeches at the beginning. And the next evening we saw clips on the news. We heard that the mayor of Lubumbashi called Kanyatsi to complain that he had been upstaged by our mayor. "After all," the mayor said, "Lubumbashi is the capitol, so things should begin in the capitol." Dr. T and I laughed. Politicians are always looking for the spotlight. The mayor of Lubumbashi wouldn't give Kanyatsi two minutes of his time before the TV coverage. Suddenly he is our supporter. Ha!

The workshop group decided that we couldn't let the ideas die. We learned so much from working with leaders from both groups. Together we had lots of ideas to rebuild Likasi. And we knew that none of our ideas would work without cooperation from both sides. We formed ourselves into the Likasi Committee for Development and Peace. I'm the secretary of the committee. It's the first time I know about that a woman has held an important position in an organization that includes men. Our bylaws require that some officers be Kassai and some be Katangese. Even the mayor asked to be a member. That gave our committee immediate status. And the mayor didn't insist on being the chairman.

Today, after only four months of work as a committee, we are celebrating our first success. Dr. T is closing the office so that the whole staff can go to the opening of the new market. Our committee, with the help of the mayor of course, has built a new market in the middle of town. It's beautiful – long cement tables for people to pile their wares on, solid floors instead of muddy trenches where the customers walk, good roofs to keep people dry in the rainy season. Katangese and Kassai have equal access to sell their goods there. All people are free to shop there. The gate to the market is decorated with a picture of clasped hands with the logo Marché de la Paix. It truly is the Market of Peace.

Odo Nnyew Fie Kwan
Love never loses its way home.

Chapter 6

Novas

Last year on my birthday I asked the white missionary lady in our build-ing if she would bake me a birthday cake. I thought maybe she would just hand me a cake that I could take home and eat with my grandma, but she invited the other kids on our street to come and have cake too. None of the kids I know in Zambia have birthday parties. It was fun. Malampi and her sisters in the apartment next door played some tapes up loud so we could hear them in the yard.

Malampi's a year older than me. She said, "Novas, now that you're eleven you can dance with the girls." She danced with me. My friend James danced with the girls too.

After the party James came to my house. James is in the same grade as me but he's a year older. Sometimes we play football together af-ter school. I showed him my new car. It's made out of wire and bottle caps.

"Wow," he said. "Where did you get such a cool car?"

"Aaron made it for me for my birthday." Aaron is Malampi's brother. He's fifteen.

"It's much cooler than the wire car I made. Mine doesn't have that extra wire on it so you can steer it just like a real car."

"I know. Aaron made it himself out of stuff he found on the street. Aaron likes to make me things, like I'm his little brother."

James said, "It's cool to have a guy like Aaron be your big brother."

The wire car is the best present I ever had. Funnest birthday party I ever had. Only one.

My grandma never has enough money for birthday cake. She doesn't have enough money to send me to private school either. But she says my school is no good. She says the teachers in government schools in Zambia only sit around and wait for the government checks instead of teaching us what we need to learn. Grandma doesn't even have enough money for my school uniforms. She makes them herself. She says she wants me to look nice even though we don't have much. She makes uniforms for some of the other boys too. The missionary lady sends her kids to the private school. All the white kids go there. Some rich black kids go there too. None I know.

I stay with Grandma because my momma died when I was born. Grandma says I was really, really sick when I was born but she took time off work for a long time until I was better. It's OK not having a mom when you have a grandma. Some of the other kids stay with aunties or older sisters because their moms or dads died. Grandma said she doesn't know where my dad is. She said she never saw him again after my momma died. He didn't even come to my momma's funeral. Grandma looked really mad when she said it. I don't know what my dad looks like. It's OK I guess.

Grandma and I live in a flat near the downtown section of Kitwe. We live in a nice part of town near the outdoor market, not like the shacks in the slums. I have my own bedroom. All of my friends have to share bedrooms and even sleep in the same bed with their brothers and sisters. But I have a bed and a whole bedroom to myself. Sometimes it's nice not having brothers and sisters. But more lonesome.

In the early morning before school I like to look out my window and see women with their bundles wrapped in bright African cloth on their heads. They're bringing tomatoes and onions they grow on their farms to sell in the market. The ones who sell dried fish are headed for another section of the market. I can smell the dried fish as they go by. The men who sell bicycle tires and wire and spare car parts are further in back.

The missionary lady lives in the flat two doors down from ours. She has books in English at her house that she lets us read. All the kids on our street come to her house and look at the books on a shelf in her sitting room. None of us have any books in our houses. Not in Bemba or in English. We bring back the books we took last time and she crosses off our names in her notebook. Then we find other books we want and tell her, and she writes those down in her notebook next to our names. The other kids forget to bring back the books, but I never do. One time the missionary lady told me to go ask Lulu where her book was. Lulu said she couldn't find the book and then she moved away. I knew she still had the book. I wouldn't do that. I want to read every book in the missionary lady's house.

One day the missionary lady showed me a tin flute. I really liked the flute. It was shiny silver and had little holes all up and down it. I'd never seen anything like it before. It must be a white thing. Zambians don't have flutes like that.

> I was so surprised when the missionary lady said, "Would you like to play it, Novas?"
>
> "Oh yes," I said.
>
> "I have a book you can read that teaches you how to play it." She showed me her book. It had some words, but mostly it had a lot of other lines and marks I've never seen.
>
> "Really? I don't know if I can."

I've never seen anyone look at a book to play music. Aaron and his friends play a keyboard and drums at church, but they only know the music they hear on tapes. All the boys think Aaron and his group are cool because they can play music. If I learned the white's music, I'd be even cooler.

> "You're a really smart boy. You like books more than all the other kids. I think you could learn," she said.
>
> No one ever told me I'm smart before. Maybe I am. So I said, "I can try."
>
> "Good. Come back tomorrow after school and we can start."

I was so excited I ran home as fast as I could to tell Grandma. I forgot to be cool and strut slow like Aaron. When I told Grandma, she had a worried look on her face. Grandma wants us to keep our backs straight. That means not accepting too much from strangers. But she said OK. I guess I can take a flute and a music book and still keep my back straight.

I really liked playing the flute. The missionary lady let me come for lessons on Tuesdays and Fridays after school. I asked her if I could come on Mondays and Thursdays too, but she said no, she was busy.

The missionary lady said I could keep the flute and the book with the music in it at my house as long as I took good care of it. I would never lose such a wonderful book. I kept it on the shelf next to my school uniform. Every day, as soon as I got home from school, I took off my uniform, and folded it and put it on the shelf, just like Grandma told me to. Then I took down the music book and my flute. Sometimes James asked me didn't I want to play football after school. Sometimes I did. But most times I played my flute. The missionary lady said I was getting really good at it.

On the first day of my school spring break, a man came to our door. He was tall, dressed in a nice suit and had a cane. He said he was my father. I was so surprised. My father coming to see me! There he was standing on our veranda.

He said, "I didn't call because your grandma doesn't have a phone. Can I come in?"

I said, "Of course. Come in and sit down." I held the door wide for my father to come in to my house. My father!

He sat down in Grandma's favorite chair and leaned his cane beside it. He told me, "I thought you would be on spring break because the kids in Lusaka, where I live, are on break now. I want you to come to my house for your spring break. Would you like to come?"

"Wow!" I said. "I've never been to Lusaka before. What's Lusaka like?"

"There's a shopping mall called Manda Hill that has lots of stores in it just like the stores in America. Much bigger than the little shops in Kitwe. I'll take you to a restaurant to eat. We can play video games."

"What are video games?"

"Games kids play on machines in the mall. I'll even buy you one we can take to my house and connect to my TV set."

"Cool. I've never been in a restaurant before."

"We have to ride on the Euro bus. It's much bigger than the minibuses you ride on in town. It takes four hours to get to Lusaka."

My grandma was at work, so we had to wait till she came home to ask her. She works all day at the YWCA teaching sewing to other women. When she came in the door and saw my father sitting in her chair, she looked kind of mad and scared all mixed together. She greeted him but didn't fix him a cup of tea or anything. She always offers visitors a cup of tea even if they're strangers.

My father asked my grandma, "How have you been, Charity?"

Grandma said, "Fine. How are you?" in a kind of tight voice.

He said, "I appreciate you taking care of Novas for me. I'd like to take him to Lusaka for spring break."

I bit my lips to keep from shouting "Yes! Oh yes, please."

Grandma sat down on another chair and said, "It's good to see you, Charles, after all these years. I didn't even know if you were still ... in Lusaka."

"Oh yes," he said. "I'm doing very well."

Grandma asked him, "Are you married?"

He said, "Yes. My wife's name is Beauty. We've been married for ten years."

"How many children do you have?"

"None yet. She's been pregnant twice, but they both died. We'll have a child soon."

Grandma seemed surprised. She asked him a lot of other things I was too excited to listen to. I kept thinking, "I have a father! *My father* has come to take me to his house in Lusaka!" I stood up extra straight so I could look tall like my father.

And then Grandma said "OK" and started packing some clothes for me to take with me.

Lusaka was great. I played video games at Manda Hill Mall and ate dinner in a real restaurant. My father told me not to eat with my hands but to eat with a fork. My father had a house with a wall around it and a guard at the gate. It was much bigger than our apartment. We rode in lots of minibuses and went to a market that is ten times bigger than our market in Kitwe. At Manda Hill Mall my father bought me a video game that connected to his TV. He said I could play it any time I wanted as long as I didn't play it too loud.

At the end of spring break my father brought me on the bus back to my grandma's house. I didn't bring the video game because my father said it wouldn't work on Grandma's TV. I was sad to leave my father. I wanted to stay in Lusaka with him and play video games all day. But I missed my grandma. Grandma cried and looked relieved when she hugged me hello.

Then, a couple of weeks after spring break my father was waiting for me when I got home from school. He was sitting in a chair on our veranda.

He said, "Pack all your clothes. You're going to live with me in Lusaka from now on." He said it just like that.

I nearly jumped up and hit the roof of the veranda. "Wowee! In Lusaka? With you? "

"Right. With me, where you belong."

While I was packing my things, I was thinking about playing video games every day! The missionary lady wasn't home so I couldn't ask her if I could take the flute with me. I left it and the book on the shelf so Grandma could give it back to her. My father wrote a note for my grandma because she wasn't home from work yet.

Living with my father was hard. I didn't get to play a flute. There were no books in my father's house. Not even one. I missed my friend James. We didn't go to any more restaurants or to Manda Hill Mall. Beauty, my father's wife, worked all day selling tomatoes for her friend in the market. She and my father yelled at each other a lot when she was home. She yelled at me too. She beat me when I didn't sweep the yard or when I didn't get good grades from school. I guess that's what wives do. I missed my grandma. My father started having more trouble walking, even with his cane. Then he had to stay in bed all day.

One day I was sitting watching TV after school and my father called me into his bedroom.

I asked, "Can I come in there? Beauty told me not to go into your room."

My father said, "Yes, you can come in now."

I had been in their house for a whole school term but I had never been in that room before. It smelled kind of old and worn out.

He talked to me in a sad, quiet voice. He said, "Novas, you have to be a man now."

I wasn't sure what he meant. But I didn't want to ask a lot of stupid-kid questions. I just said, "OK."

He kind of whispered, "I want you to be proud of me."

I told him, "You're my father."

The next day he died.

People at the funeral whispered that he died of a long term illness, but I didn't think he was sick that long. His wife said she couldn't take care of me any more so I had to go back and live with my grandma. She asked her brother to take me on the bus to Kitwe.

Grandma looked surprised and burst into tears when she saw me come in the door. She hugged me for a long, long time.

She said, "I thought I would never see you again."

"My father died," I said. I tried to keep my back straight and not cry.

"I know. I heard about it. I'm glad Beauty let you come back."

"She said it was your job to take care of me, not hers."

Grandma knelt down and looked me straight in the eyes. She said, "I want to take care of you, Novas. I love you."

I hugged her really hard. That was the first time anyone ever told me that.

I told Malampi about my father and she said he died of AIDS. James came over that first day and we played football. The missionary lady came over and said we can start flute lessons again next week.

I'm glad to be home.

Ese Ne Tekrema
The teeth and the tongue
Symbol of friendship and interdependence
The teeth and the tongue play interdependent roles in the mouth.
They may come into conflict, but they
need to work together.

Chapter 7

Issa

I wake to yet another boring day in this prison without walls called Maheba Refugee Settlement. I am only a few kilometers away from Congo, my home country. The hills look the same, the air feels the same. But mountains of prejudice and war stand between me and home.

Odila, the young man down the street, finds ways to go to the border every few weeks. He sneaks out the back gate with two goats on the back of his bicycle and returns with bicycles to sell to other refugees. He tells me, "Issa, you should come too. You can make money that way. It's better than waiting forever for the Zambian government to pay you what they owe you for teaching in their schools." But he just visits Congo. I don't want to visit.

Home is the house where I was born, the ground where my umbilical cord is buried, the place I can only visit in my dreams. Home is a village where my parents go every Sunday to a small church. There is no mosque.

After I became a follower of Allah, I went to Friday prayers in my friend's sitting room. Only a few of us could fit our prayer rugs between the furniture. After I changed my name to Issa, I could never go home again. This refugee camp is home for no one, yet 50,000 people stay here.

Home is in a country that used to be. It is no more. Home is a village where people of different tribes and different religions live side by side in harmony. Home is where neighbors are aunts and uncles to children even through no blood ties them together. Home is a place where people work together and celebrate births together and grieve the dead together. Where neighbors take five more children into their homes after their parents die of AIDS. Home is a place where there is no war.

The imam in our village taught me the Qur'an forbids people to kill. When the fighting came near to our village we heard rumors that all the young men were being captured by rebels and forced to be soldiers. If you escaped the rebels, the other side would find you. They took every man and boy in every village they came to. I couldn't be a soldier. I had a good job teaching *maths* in the school in our village. It tore my heart out to think of my students being handed guns and forced to kill people. I could not take a life when I had worked so hard to nourish life. I said goodbye to my parents and started walking towards Zambia.

It was a long walk. I met others on the way, young men like me, but also mothers with babies on their backs, leading small children by the hand. They had their whole lives in bundles on their heads. I had mine in a cardboard box. I sometimes helped them cross rivers. Soldiers were waiting on the bridges. We never knew if they were rebels or government soldiers. We just knew that they would grab every boy and man and force them to fight their war. They might do even worse to the women. So we had to find logs to build rafts to get across the rivers. None of us knew how to swim and sometimes the water was deep. Some of them didn't make it. I helped the young ones keep walking when their mothers fell.

As our group got closer to the border, we saw more and more people. Some had worn out their shoes and were walking barefoot. Most
had used up or lost everything on the journey and were walking with
empty hands. Everyone was hungry. Babies were too tired to cry. I
helped carry young children I had never seen before. The guards at the
border waved us on through. They had seen many like us before.

UN High Commission for Refugees (UNHCR) had set up a table in a
small hut just over the border. People waited patiently in line because
we knew we were safely across to the Zambian side. They put us in
buses for the few miles to Meheba Refugee Settlement.

When I came to the camp, UNHCR gave me mud bricks and neighbors helped me build this house. After I got a job teaching *maths* at
Meheba Secondary School, I bought a couch and a bed. When Mary
and I were married she moved in her table and chairs. Gradually we
made this house a home for the two of us. Mary is Zambian. We met
when she came to work in the school. She's in her home country, but
she would have to leave me here if she wanted to live outside the camp.
Married to me, she has become a refugee in her own country.

Mary was a Christian when I met her. I was surprised that she would
be interested in having a relationship with a Muslim like me. My own
family didn't even accept my conversion to Islam. They thought I was
crazy to change my name and the beliefs that our family had accepted
for generations. But Mary said she loved me and it didn't matter what
her family said. She said it didn't matter what name we called God. God
is the same God. At that moment I asked her to marry me. I knew then
that we could survive any problems.

We've been married for 7 years, Mary and I. From the beginning I
have hoped Allah would bless us with a child. But Mary has heart problems. We lost three babies before they could be born. My family told
me, "Send her away. If she can't give you children, you should give her

back to her parents." I refused. Mary and I love each other. We are married in the sight of God. I won't send her away. A doctor told us to stop trying to have a child for a couple of years until Mary built up her strength. So we did. It was hard to wait. Both of our families put a lot of pressure on us. They shamed us, told us it was our duty to the family to keep trying to have children. And finally our waiting paid off.

Five months ago our daughter Miracle was born. She is beautiful and healthy. Mary is strong enough to nurse her, but every month we need to make the seven-hour bus trip to Lusaka for doctor's visits to make sure Mary is doing OK. The bus trip is long and hard on her. It's always difficult to get passes to travel out of the camp.

It would be much easier if we could live in Lusaka, but I'm not sure it's worth the risk. There are lots of Congolese and Rwandan refugees living illegally in Lusaka. The laws in Zambia require all refugees to live in camps far from the cities. There are no exceptions.

My friend Thomas is a veterinarian. His wife is a teacher. They couldn't stand doing nothing but farming nine hundred kilometers from everywhere. So they sell bicycle parts and tomatoes in the markets in Lusaka and take their chances. Last Christmas Eve the police broke down their door and put them in jail. There were more than two hundred refugees rounded up that night. The police dragged them out with their children clinging to their legs. After Catholic Commission for Justice and Peace got them released and sent them here, they stayed overnight with us and caught the next bus to Lusaka. I don't know if Mary's heart could take that kind of stress.

Last year some people came from Mindolo Ecumenical Foundation, a college in Kitwe, to do a training. They called it Messengers of Peace. Most people here sign up for any kind of class just to relieve the boredom. I have my teaching job to keep me busy most of the time, but I thought this class would be useful in my work with students. They put us to work in the camp settling problems with neighbors. We Congolese had to learn to work with Angolans, our traditional enemies, in order to make peace in the camp.

At the end of the training the trainers put us in groups with Angolans and told us to talk about what we liked about Angolans and what we didn't like. The Angolans had to say what they liked about Congolese and what they didn't like. At first there was this dead silence. I didn't know whether to laugh or to speak up. No one wanted to say what we were all thinking. We all know that Angolans think that Congolese cheat and steal and that we hate the Angolans being in charge of everything and not letting Congolese have a chance. I decided to say it out loud.

I looked directly at Zuze. He's Angolan and has been in Meheba since he was a teenager. He now has teenagers of his own. He teaches at Meheba Secondary School where I teach. He's a lot taller than me, as most Angolans are.

> I looked up at him and said. "I think the Angolans should give ladders to all the Congolese so we can look down on them like they looked down on us for years." Everybody laughed.

> Then Zuze said, "I think the Congolese should give sunglasses to the Angolans so we can shield their eyes from your bright clothes and flashy jewelry."

I am my enemy and my enemy is me. After that the whole group started to work together. Zuze and I came up with a project to help girls in our school support each other in resisting sexual advances from "sugar daddies."

The trainers from Kitwe came back a couple of months later and trained a smaller group of us to do the training in other refugee camps.

I saw a chance to get out of Meheba and to meet with Congolese from other areas. Don't get me wrong. I'm grateful for my teaching job. It's a lot better than the jobs most people at Meheba have. But I don't want to be teaching maths to refugee kids for the rest of my life.

In the training we learned new methods of adult education, very different from the memorization we use in school. We learned to analyze conflict situations in the camp and figure out what strategies would work best in each situation. I'd like to teach these skills in Congo, if I ever get the chance to go back.

The people in charge of the training insisted that the training include as many women as men. That was difficult. It's hard to change the ways we're all used to. Some people quote scripture to keep from changing. Tango was on our team. She doesn't even know how to read very well. Why should she get to be a teacher if she hasn't even had more than a year or two of school herself? But we had to accept the women, two of them on each team of four. We got bicycles to ride around the camp. You're somebody if you have a bicycle. Tango didn't know how to ride a bicycle because her family didn't let girls do such things. Tango let others ride her bicycle. Actually I found out that Tango is a good trainer. She speaks up for other women and she notices things that people are afraid to talk about. I've learned a lot from Tango.

The training for trainers was really good for us all to learn to work together, Angolans and Congolese. One of the groups even made up a skit about Americans stirring up trouble in Africa. We all looked sideways at the white American woman who was in charge of the training to see if she would laugh. She did. We were relieved.

It was good to be sent as a trainer to other refugee camps. I was looked up to as a teacher so they accepted my different name and religion. We even went to the camp for Angolan ex-soldiers, Ukwimi. It's where UNHCR puts people who admit they were soldiers before they came. There are quite a few men in Meheba who were soldiers but who lied about it when they came across the border. It was only the ones who admitted it that were sent to Ukwimi.

The UN was getting ready to close the camp and force everyone to go back to Angola. Anna is in that camp too. She's a Burundian woman who is Tutsi and married to a Hutu man. She used to be in Meheba but had a lot of problems because her husband's family was there too and they shunned her because of her tribe. Her husband treated her badly too.

In Ukwimi I suggested to the other trainers that we try starting the training with sessions on trauma healing because these refugees have suffered even more trauma than most refugees. The other trainers agreed. It was amazing. The people really opened up. Those who had given false names to the UN to cover up their past wanted their graduation certificates written in their true names so they could work with people back home. They were ready to teach them what they had learned about healing old wounds. I was pleased when the white American woman in charge of the program praised the changes we had made in the training. She told the UN funders what a good job we had done. The UN people even asked for a list of all the people we had trained so the UN could use the refugees as peacebuilders in Angola.

After we trained people in all the other camps in Zambia, we had to come back and do nothing in Meheba. So Odila, Jean Kabengele and I and some others decided we should keep on training people as Messengers of Peace. We didn't have anything else better to do and it might help us get some more UN funding. So we got UNHCR to let us use a building and started holding classes. Just like us, other refugees were bored and needed something to do, so they signed up for the classes. We formed our own Non-Governmental Organization, Meheba Messengers of Peace, MEMOP. We just kept having classes and sending more and more people out into the camp to find the conflicts and do something about them instead of just complaining. We got the people from Kitwe to come up for graduation, which made people notice us all the more. And more and more people kept signing up.

Mary's health didn't improve much and we needed to move to Lusaka. So I talked to the Mennonite Central Committee and got them to fund my salary as a conflict resolution teacher in schools. Our little family of three is now legally in Lusaka. Mary doesn't have to be a refugee anymore and our little Miracle is a Zambian citizen. Maybe that village in Congo where my umbilical cord is buried isn't really home anymore.

Issa and his family are now living in Lusaka. He is the executive director of Peace Club, a non-profit organization sponsored by the Mennonite Central Committee which has created clubs in 26 schools in Zambia to teach conflict transformation to students. He has trained more than 1,000 students to be peacemakers.

Hwe Mu Dua
Measuring stick
Symbol of examination and quality control
This symbol stresses the need to strive for the best
quality, whether in production of goods or
in human endeavors

Chapter 8

Patience

It was just a gentle bump, not hard enough to bend either car's bumper, but enough to irritate the driver in front. The two women, one black, one white, sat in the car waiting in traffic for the light to change. The usual children in the middle of the street leaned into the car windows to sell their wares—baseball caps, oranges, shorts, plastic toys, pineapples, cell-phone chargers, dress shirts.

In spite of the heat, Lois, in the passenger seat, rolled up her window to shut out their dirty faces and their pleading eyes. Her blond hair and white skin always made her an object of curiosity and marked her as a potential customer for the street vendors on the streets of Lusaka. As she watched, the car slowly inched forward. If Patience didn't put her foot on the brake soon, they would run into the car ahead of them. Lois didn't want to insult Patience by telling her how to drive. After all it was Patience who had cut through the miles of red tape to get Lois, and her husband Rob, Zambian drivers' licenses when they arrived four months before. Patience had driven in this kind of traffic for years. So Lois sat in silence waiting for the impact.

"Oh, did I do that?" Patience was jerked back to reality.

"Yes, but it wasn't serious," replied Lois.

The light changed to green. The driver in the other car scowled into his rear-view mirror and moved ahead.

Lois and Rob Myers had moved from Canada to work for the Mennonite Central Committee (MCC) in Africa almost two decades previously. Their daughter Alicia had been born in Congo when they worked there as economic development assistants. Their son James was born four years later when they were in South Africa. Now the kids were teenagers and adjusting to boarding schools while their parents started their term as Mennonite Central Committee country representatives for Zambia, managing twelve volunteers scattered throughout the country.

It was just a little bump. It could have happened to anyone. We have all been lost in thought enough to let a foot slip off the brake pedal waiting for the light to change. So Lois never mentioned it to anyone until much later. Afterwards she realized this was the beginning.

After she finished high school, Patience had been selected by the Mennonite Central Committee as the only young woman to be included in a post-high-school exchange program to the U.S. She had graduated at the top of her class. There were several young men in Solwezi, her home village, who proposed marriage to keep her from going to the U.S. But Patience knew that, in spite of her ordinary appearance and her darker brown skin, America would make her more marriageable, not less. She spent a year in Cincinnati working in a thrift shop and living with a Mennonite family. When she returned to Zambia, she had grown decades beyond her three older sisters and her brother. Try as they might, the arms of her parents and relatives in Solwezi were too flimsy to hold her back. She graduated at the top of her class in secretarial school in Lusaka, the capital. When MCC needed a secretary, she was easily the first on the list.

When Lois and Rob arrived as the new managers of the Zambia program, they were very pleased to find Patience as their secretary to help them navigate the intricacies of life in their new country. Rob's skills as a carpenter and his large, generous hugs were welcome additions to the office and to their house in one of Lusaka's middle class neighborhoods. Lois's open smile welcomed in the many people from local non-profits constantly looking for assistance from MCC.

Patience had the office skills necessary to keep the office running when Lois and Rob traveled around Zambia. Her familiarity with MCC from her U.S. experience was an added bonus. After two years in the office, Lois and Rob offered to help her buy one of the council houses that the government was selling at very cheap prices. Overwhelmed at their generosity, Patience gratefully accepted. A young single woman homeowner was unheard of in her social circles, even in all of Zambia.

Out of loyalty, Patience still attended the same Brethren in Christ Church in Lusaka and sang in the choir, but her enthusiasm was diminishing. Her friends from secretarial school wanted her to come to the Anglican Church with them, where she could meet better husband material. After all, she was approaching thirty and still unmarried. She should be on an all-out quest for a ring on her left hand. But Patience clung to the Brethren in Christ.

Patience was the envy of her friends. She owned a house. It was in a poorer section of town without paved streets but it was hers. She had a job with an NGO, a much more stable position than any with a Zambian company. She had a car, like white people or rich Zambians did, and didn't have to depend on public transportation, small vans with their doors falling off that had to be pushed to start. It was a great luxury to drive herself to work. She could arrive neatly pressed instead of having her skirt squashed into a bedraggled lump by the fifteen passengers required to be packed into a van designed to carry twelve.

She had it all. Except for a husband. Actually she didn't really want a husband. She knew her friends' husbands stayed out late drinking and often found other women's beds more comfortable than their own. She knew the AIDS statistics. The rate of her own friends' dying told her that the HIV infection rate was much higher than the official 12%. The fact that two out of her five sisters and one of her brothers had died of this "long term illness" was an indication. What could a husband give her but trouble?

But her mother kept at her. "When are you going to find a husband? How can you shame me like this? Thirty and not even engaged."

And her friends, especially the married ones, always rolled their eyes at her. "How can you ever be happy without a man?" "You're not a real woman until you're married." "You *are* a real woman, aren't you?"

Lois assured her that women in Canada and the U.S. commonly wait until after thirty to marry. That AIDS had changed the rules for marriage. But Lois's voice was foreign in Zambia.

So when her friends pushed her in the direction of Charles, the new fellow at the Lusaka Brethren in Christ Church, she was too tired to resist. Charles was tall, good looking, more milk-chocolate than dark coffee brown, which made him more desirable as a mate. He always sat in the back row in church and perused the young women in the choir. He had a job. He was a mechanic at Kitwe Road Garage. Yes, he had sown his wild oats in his younger days, but he found Jesus and joined the church. So he was about as safe as possible.

They were married in a quiet church ceremony in Solwezi. It wasn't the twenty bridesmaids and a dinner in a hotel her friends in Lusaka wanted. Just what her savings account could manage. They borrowed tables from the church, and all the women from the village came to help cook a goat, cabbage and three pots of *nshima*, the staple food no meal in Zambia is complete without. Her mother sewed her dress from fabric Patience bought in Lusaka. Her aunts and high school friends feted her with a traditional *matebeto* ceremony, cooking every traditional food and teaching her the lessons of married life until the early hours of the morning.

The happy couple went home to her house in Lusaka, and she went back to work. Charles couldn't get more than a weekend off from his job. She was ready for the wedded bliss her friends had promised.

Her new husband didn't go out drinking with his buddies too many nights after work. He was usually home within a couple of hours after closing time. He didn't complain too much about her cooking. Patience was able to convince him she really did know how to cook all those dishes her matron of honor served him at the *matebeto* ceremony. When she asked her friends, they said as far as they knew he wasn't in some other woman's bed. Yet. Life was about as good as it was going to get. Until Charles got sick.

Patience thought he was just working too hard, trying too hard to prove to her that he could buy a car as nice as hers. But then she began noticing the sores that wouldn't heal and the weakness in his legs.

One Thursday Charles' boss called Patience at work. "I think you need to come and get Charles. He needs to go to the hospital."

Knowing the inevitable, but desperately praying it wasn't true, Patience replied, "I'll be right there." No panic. No confusion. Her only thought was, "Thank God I didn't get pregnant."

By Monday he was dead. Five months after their first anniversary. The "long term illness" was short this time. They told the mourners he died of malaria.

Patience went back to business as usual. She was sorry that Charles had died. A human life, a child of God, had left this earth. He was as good a friend as a man can be to a woman. She refused to consider the question of whether he was in heaven or not. Her life returned to normal. And now she was a widow. She had status in the community. She joined the ranks of millions of widows under forty in Africa.

She didn't even notice her own symptoms because they were so different from those she had seen in Charles. Lois found it harder and harder to explain her mental lapses at work. Patience broke her own rule again!st her family moving in with her. She was too tired to cook dinner after dragging herself home every evening after work. So she allowed her niece Beatrice to live with her while Beatrice was going to nursing school. She told her family she was doing Beatrice a favor.

> About a year after Charles died Beatrice called Lois at home one evening. "Mama Lois, please come and get Patience."

> Lois was puzzled. "What's wrong Beatrice?"

> "Patience is acting strange."

> "What's she doing?"

> "She sees what's not there."

> "Beatrice, I don't understand. What do you mean?"

"Just come quickly, Mama Lois."

When Beatrice answered the door she had to grab Patience's arm to keep her from running out. Lois grabbed the other arm and together they dragged the protesting Patience back into the house. Patience continued to insist that her relatives were just outside the window putting money for her in a bush.

Alarmed, Lois said, "I'm glad you called me Beatrice. Patience, can you sit down for a few minutes while I'm talking to Beatrice?"

Patience peered out the window. "They're right there. I can see them."

Beatrice sat down next to Lois and burst into tears. "I don't know what to do with her, Mama Lois. What is happening to her?"

Patience insisted, "They put money in that bush. I have to go out and get it."

Lois put her hand on Beatrice's arm and tried to calm Patience at the same time. "I'm not sure, but I can see that it's something very serious."

"Let me go!" Patience screamed.

"Beatrice, can you come along with me to help me get her to the hospital?"

"Yes, I'll get our coats."

"Bring along Patience's pajamas too."

Patience screamed, "They're coming! They're coming!"

Patience hurriedly and willingly put on her coat. "Yes, yes. Here we go."

With Lois and Beatrice on either side, they detoured Patience from the bush and pushed her into the back seat of Lois's car. Patience pressed her face to the window searching frantically. Only Lois's control of the locks on the back doors kept Patience inside as they sped off.

Lois phoned Rob as soon as they made it to a street with streetlights. "Patience is having delusions. The hospital probably won't have any secure place to keep her. What do you think about bringing her to our house until the clinic opens in the morning?"

Rob's heart was a big as his frame. "Bring her here and we'll figure out something."

Lois began to sing Sunday School songs in Nyanja that she hoped Patience would remember from childhood. Beatrice joined in and put her arms around Patience. By the time they reached the Myers' home, Patience was snuggled in Beatrice's arms humming along.

As soon as Lois beeped the horn at the locked gate, Rob was waiting to let them in. Patience's demons stirred again as soon as she saw Rob. But his extra height and strength helped get Patience into the house. The guest rooms they kept for volunteers and friends traveling through were empty, so they had space for Patience in a room with 2 single beds. Beatrice was given a separate room.

Lois's hopes for even part of a night's sleep vanished after she sang every lullaby she could remember or invent, in English, Nyanja and several other languages, and Patience still stood on the bed screaming, terrified of the people she saw in the darkness outside. Finally Lois handed out to Beatrice coat hangers, small objects, and everything else in the room that might be dangerous. Then she carefully slipped out, locking the door behind her. Patience's screams still reverberated in waves, but some hours later she fell exhausted to the floor.

The next morning, before the receptionist could get the key out of the clinic door, Lois, Beatrice and Rob ushered Patience to the clinic waiting room. Dr. Chung, the best AIDS consultant in Lusaka, admitted Patience to Lusaka General but held out no hope. Dr. Chung confirmed that in some cases the time between exposure to AIDS and death can be as short as 13 months.

Patience died a week later. Her parents told everyone she died of malaria. A few of her friends and members of the choir began to rethink their advice that a woman must be married, no matter what the cost.

Hye Won Hye
That which does not burn
Symbol of imperishability and endurance
This symbol gets its meaning from traditional priests that were able
to walk on fire without burning their feet, an inspiration to others to
endure and overcome difficulties.

Chapter 9

The Dag Hammarskjöld
Messengers of Peace Program

The Dag Hammarskjöld Messengers of Peace and Good Governance program began on the campus of Mindolo Ecumenical Foundation, a small community college in Kitwe, Zambia as a project teaching conflict resolution skills to community leaders in Zambia. It soon expanded to include a workshop bringing together women from diverse religious groups — Christian, Muslim and Baha'i, in Zambia and neighboring Democratic Republic of Congo, (D.R. Congo) — and another training for senior officers of the Zambian police force.

The idea for the Messengers of Peace in refugee camps was planted by Mindolo Ecumenical Foundation students, Quentin Kanyatsi and Jose Noé. Kanyatsi, from D.R. Congo, and Noé, from Angola, were students in the Peacebuilding and Conflict Transformation program. The two had been sent to Meheba Refugee Settlement in northern Zambia for their six-week fieldwork assignment in June, 2000. Meheba was the refugee settlement in Zambia that housed primarily Angolan and

Congolese refugees. As part of their fieldwork they led conflict transformation workshops with refugees. They quickly discovered that refugees were delighted to have some productive activity, especially when it related to resolving disputes. Kanyatsi and Noé returned to campus with requests from many of the refugees for more peacebuilding programs. In order to enroll at Mindolo, refugees would need scholarships. Scholarships were in very limited supply. It made better sense to take the programs to the students.

DeEtte Beghtol, coordinator of the Peacebuilding program at Mindolo, took the idea to Olubanke King Akerele, head of UN programs in Zambia. Would the U.N. be willing to fund a program to teach refugees peacebuilding skills? The programs could help settle disputes in the refugee camps as well as prepare refugees for building peace as they returned to their home countries. Ms. King Akerele liked the idea enough to begin funding it out of her own budget until U.N. High Commission for Refugees (UNHCR) took it up.

The program began in Meheba Refugee Settlement, the largest of eight refugee camps and settlements in Zambia, with a week of classroom instruction designed to identify conflicts in the camp and to create specific action plans to address them. Teams of participants had a month to implement their action plans before the trainers came back for another week of class, followed by another month of implementation. This pattern was repeated for six months before a final graduation. Each monthly class began with an evaluation of the action plans and suggestions for improvement or modification. At the refugees' request, the trainers added study of the UN Convention on the Rights of Refugees and other official documents that impacted the civil rights of the participants. Participants were not granted a certificate of completion unless they had worked with the action plans as well as the classes.

The UNHCR in Zambia was so pleased with the results of the Meheba training they decided to take the program to the rest of the camps and settlements. The coordinators from Mindolo selected twenty of the graduates from the first course to be trained as trainers for other camps. The use of refugees themselves as trainers was key to the success of the rest of the program. Refugees did not need translators and already knew the types of conflicts their fellow refugees suffered. Refugee trainers met after each week of class with coordinators at Mindolo for evaluation and future planning.

These evaluations and the feedback from the refugee trainers led to the discovery that trauma healing is an integral part of conflict transformation for refugees. A Trauma Healing module was added to the course. This module turned out to be the most important part of the course. Trainers discovered that if refugees have a chance to talk to others about the trauma they have suffered, then almost all conflicts are easier to resolve.

The last group to be trained as Messengers of Peace was at Ukwimi, a camp that had been set aside for ex-combatants. Some refugees in this camp had given UNHCR false names because they didn't want to admit to being participants in wars. After the training the new Messengers of Peace had a dilemma: they wanted their true names to be listed on their graduation certificates as proof of their changed ways, but they were afraid to let UNHCR know their true identities. Angolans were eager to return home to work with UN agencies to resolve conflicts between returning refugees and those who remained during the war, but they would need their true names on their certificates. So the refugee trainers submitted parallel lists to the coordinators at Mindolo. One name was on the official certificate and a second name was on the outside envelope and the announcement at the graduation ceremony. The coordinators winked at the subterfuge, pleased that the new Messengers of Peace would return home eager to be peacebuilders instead of combatants.

After Messengers of Peace were trained in all the camps in Zambia, the original group in Meheba was not content to rest. They could see that every refugee, not just a small group, needed training in conflict transformation. They began organizing trainings without outside funding, asking trainers to volunteer their time and obtaining space and materials from other organizations working within Meheba. They formed themselves into Meheba Messengers of Peace – MEMOP – their own non-profit organization. They trained their own trainers, who trained still more Messengers of Peace, spreading to every zone of the settlement.

Meheba Messengers of Peace continues to transform conflicts and to train others in the Meheba Refugee Settlement. Most of the other refugee camps in Zambia have now been closed. The remaining refugees have been moved to Meheba, which now houses about 10,000 refugees from Angola, Congo, Rwanda, Burundi and Sudan. Conflicts increased when refugees from warring countries were forced to be neighbors. MEMOP rose to these new challenges, and continues to intervene and prevent violence. In recent years FORGE, (see their website at www.FORGEnow.org) a U.S.-based non-profit which uses youth volunteers to develop programs for refugees in Zambia, has supported MEMOP in continuing to train refugee peacebuilders.

At last report there are now more than 10,000 Messengers of Peace in Africa spreading peace.

Appendix A

The Life of a Refugee in Zambia

What is life like for a refugee? What does a refugee do when she cannot return to her homeland without risking rape or death, and cannot move beyond the guarded gate of a refugee camp?

Refugees in Zambia, in south-central Africa, fled civil wars in their homelands. They came from the neighboring countries of Angola and Congo, but also from Rwanda, Burundi, and Sudan. They were granted refugee status by the UN High Commission for Refugees (UNHCR) because they had left their homeland and had legitimate reasons to fear returning. Until wars stopped in their countries, UNHCR provided them with food and a place to live. Those living in camps were fed and housed until it was safe to return home. Those living in settlements, where land was available, were given a half-acre of ground to till. They were supported for two years and then expected to become self-sustaining unless they were disabled or were children without guardians.

Sometimes camp authorities would assign young children who were orphaned or without guardians to women without asking their permission. An official would simply arrive at a woman's doorstep and deposit the child.

So, in Zambia at least, the answer to the question, "What does he do?" is "He raises sweet potatoes." The reality is he sits and is bored much of the time. It doesn't matter if he is a veterinarian or if she is a skilled worker or businessperson, the only occupation is farming. Medical doctors are the exception to the rule. The Zambian government has a shortage of doctors, so the very few refugees who are doctors are given jobs. The rest make do with farming.

Farming itself is restricted by the market. The only market available to refugees is selling to a select number of truckers who come into the settlement at harvest time. Prices are fixed by the trucker and are always lower than farmers can obtain on the other side of the gate. But refugees are not allowed to take their produce outside the settlement. Many refugees have little interest in this sort of farming.

Because Meheba Refugee Settlement is close to the Congo border, a few people regularly sneak out the back path with a goat loaded on the back of a bicycle. They pedal more than 20 miles to the nearest town on the other side of the border. There they trade the goat for another bicycle and return to the refugee settlement to sell it, a reasonably profitable import-export business.

Those refugees not wishing to be farmers have the choice of living illegally outside the camps or finding other means of earning a living. Those who live illegally outside the camps are subject to random raids on their homes, jail and transport back to the camps. One such raid occurred on Christmas Eve in Zambia's capital Lusaka. Police cars suddenly appeared in neighborhoods well known as refugee neighborhoods and carted more than 200 people to jail. Most of them, after being transported to the refugee camps, promptly left the camp again illegally, boarded buses and returned to Lusaka.

For a refugee in Zambia it is not possible to escape the camp by marrying a Zambian. Zambian spouses have to move into the camp in order to live with their husbands or wives. Children born on Zambian soil in the camp are not allowed to become Zambian citizens. Yet they usually are not citizens of the country of their parents. The question of their civil rights and citizenship remains unanswered.

The Zambian government declared these restrictions to be "exceptions" to the UN Convention on the Rights of Refugees. According to UN regulations, the country agreeing to host refugees has a right to decide which sections of the Convention it will accept and which it will not. The document designed to establish refugees' rights is redefined by each host country. Refugees are caught in the middle with limited rights.

Within the camp or settlement, refugees have very little access to health care. Meheba Refugee Settlement has a small "clinic" to care for those with tuberculosis or AIDS. A refugee with any other health problem has to obtain a day pass to leave the settlement to seek medical care in Solwezi, about 20 miles away. It is up to the refugee to pay for whatever services are provided.

Refugees in Zambia are generally unhappy being forced to live in these "prisons without walls." Organizations designed to help refugees, such as Jesuit Refugee Service (www.jrs.net) and FORGE (www.FORGEnow.org), provide services, but have no power to make substantial changes. Many refugees from Angola and Congo have returned to their home countries. About 10,000 remain at Meheba.

Appendix B

Peace Organizations in Africa

Africa has many people working for peace in their local communities. I list here some of the larger organizations.

Africa Peacebuilding and Reconciliation Resources
Hizkias Assefa
P.O. Box 63560-00619, Nairobi, Kenya
Tel: 254-20-387-2639 or 254-734-232-685
Fax: 254-20-387-4888
hizkias.assefa09@gmail.com

African Centre for the Constructive Resolution of Disputes (ACCORD)
Tel: 27 31-502 3908
Fax: 27 31-502 4160
http:// www.accord.org.za/
info@accord.org.za

American Friends Service Committee
Dereje Wordofa
Africa Regional Office
P.O. Box 66448-00800, Nairobi, Kenya
Tel: 215-241-7168
http://www.afsc.org/africa
ipafrica@afsc.org

Catholic Commission for Justice and Peace (Malawi)
The Coordinator
CCJP-Lilongwe Diocese
P/Bag A208, Lilongwe, Malawi
Tel: 265-017-66484 or 265-017-66487
Cell: 09-27-0660
justice-peace@malawi.net

Centre for Peace Initiatives in Africa

P.O. Box 7370, Harare, Zimbabwe
Physical address : Centre for Peace Initiatives in Africa
5 Corrine Close, Bluffhill, Harare
Tel: 263-4-293-2645 or 263-4-293-2646
http://www.cpia.org.zw
rchitombo@yahoo.com

Mindolo Ecumenical Foundation

Box 21493, Kitwe, Zambia
Tel: 260-221-4572
Fax: 260-221-1001
http://www.globalministries.org/africa/partners/mindolo-ecumenical-foundation.html
Annually hosts Africa Peacebuilding Institute

Nairobi Peace Initiative - Africa

P.O. Box 14894-00800, Nairobi, Kenya
Tel: (Nairobi) 254-20-444-1444 or 254-20-444-0098
Fax: 254-20-444-0097
http://www.npi-africa.org/
info@npi-africa.org

Quaker Peace
Centre (Capetown, South Africa)

3 Rye Road, Mowbray, Cape Town, 7700 South Africa
Tel: 27-21-685-7800
Fax: 27-21-685-8167
http://capetown.quaker.org
qpc@qpc.org.za

Quaker Peace Initiatives in Africa

The African Great Lakes Initiative (AGLI)
(For Burundi, Congo, Kenya, Rwanda, Tanzania and Uganda)
David Zarembka
P.O. Box 189, Kipkaren River, 50241 Kenya
Tel: 254-(0)-726-590-783
Dave@aglifpt.org
or

Friends Peace Teams
1001 Park Avenue, St. Louis, MO 63104 USA
Dawn Rubbert
Tel: 314-647-1287 (Main office in St. Louis, MO)
Dawn@aglifpt.org

University for Peace - Africa
Addis Ababa Office:
Address: UPEACE Africa Programme
P.O. Box 2794 Code 1250, Addis Ahaba, Ethiopia.
Tel: 251-11-618-0991
Fax: 251-11-618-0993
http://www.africa.upeace.org/contact.cfm
africaprogramme@upeace.org

West Africa Network for Peacebuilding (WANEP)
Physical address:
C542/18 Ashiakle Street Extension, Abelemkpe, Ghana
Postal address:
P.O. Box CT 4434, Cantonment-Accra, Ghana
Tel: 233-30-277-5975 or 233-30-277-5977 or 233-30-277-5981
Fax: 233-30-277-6018
http://www.wanep.org
wanep@wanep.org

1. Gyawu Atiko 2. Akoma ntoaso 3. Epa 4. Nkyimkyim 5. Nsirewa 6. Nsa
7. Mpuannum 8. Duafe 9. Nkuruma kese 10. Aya 11. Aban 12. Nkotimsefuopua
13. Sankofa 14. Sankofa 15. Kuntinkantan 16. Epa (see page 114 for translations)

Appendix C

Adinkra Symbols

The symbols at the beginning of each chapter of this book are Adinkra symbols from West Africa. They are part of a rich tradition of hundreds of symbols which were developed by the Ashante people and can be traced back to the 17th century. Each symbol represents a concept or aphorism. There are many different symbols with distinct meanings, often linked with proverbs.

The symbols have a decorative function but also represent objects that encapsulate evocative messages that convey traditional wisdom, aspects of life or the environment.

In earlier times clothes adorned with Adinkra symbols were only worn during ceremonies to honor the dead. The symbols worn on the mourner's clothing expressed the qualities s/he attributed to the deceased. Over time, the number of symbols grew. In modern times, they are used for every-day wear, as well as for special occasions.

They were first used as decorative elements on highly valued, hand-printed and hand-embroidered cloths of West Africa. Traditionally the cloth was used exclusively by royalty and spiritual leaders for very important sacred ceremonies and rituals.

Today the symbols are used extensively in fabrics, pottery, logos and advertising and carved on stools for domestic and ritual use. They are incorporated into walls and other architectural features.

Fabric adinkra are often made by woodcut sign writing as well as screen printing. Adinkra symbols appear on some traditional Akan gold weights. Tourism has led to new departures in the use of the symbols in such items as T-shirts and jewelry.

The Adinkra symbols shown here were recorded by Robert Sutherland Rattray, Religion and Art in Ashanti (Oxford, 1927).

1. Gyawu Atiko, lit. the back of Gyawu's head. Gyawu was a sub-chief of Bantama who at the annual Odwira ceremony is said to have had his hair shaved in this fashion.

2. Akoma ntoaso, lit. the joined hats.
3. Epa, handcuffs. See also No. 16.
4. Nkyimkyim, the twisted pattern.
5. Nsirewa, cowries.
6. Nsa, from a design of this name found on nsa cloths.
7. Mpuannum, lit. five tufts (of hair).
8. Duafe. the wooden comb.
9. Nkuruma kese, lit. dried okros.
10. Aya, the fern; the word also means 'I am not afraid of you', 'I am independent of you' and the wearer may imply this by wearing it.
11. Aban, a two-storied house, a castle; this design was formerly worn by the King of Ashanti alone.
12. Nkotimsefuopua, certain attendants on the Queen Mother who dressed their hair in this fashion. It is really a variation of the swastika.
13. Sankofa, lit. turn back and fetch it.
14. Sankofa, (another version) lit. turn back and fetch it.
15. Kuntinkantan, lit. bent and spread out ; nkuntinkantan is used in the sense of ' do not boast, do not be arrogant '.
16. Epa, handcuffs, same as No. 3.

The Author

DeEtte Beghtol Waleed says that Africa changed her life. Her six years teaching peacebuilding in Zambia created new lenses for her to see the world. She experienced a myriad of African cultures through her students from many war-torn countries who came to Zambia to learn how to lead their communities to peace.

Messengers of Peace, her first book of creative nonfiction, contains stories of collaborators in peacebuilding, ordinary individuals working in diverse ways to make the world more peaceful.

Waleed has been a peace activist and community organizer for more than 20 years. She believes that we learn best by sharing our personal journeys with each other. She teaches at Portland State University in Portland, Oregon, where she lives with her partner.